KT-384-380

Six for Texas

When Tom Nation was lynched for no good reason there was only Ed Colerich left alive to take the word back to the T Bar N on the Brightwater. So when six rode back to Texas, they only had two things on their minds: an eye for an eye and a tooth for a tooth. With guns blazing and blood flowing there wasn't one man or woman among them certain to return to the T Bar N alive. . . .

By the same author

The Brothers Gant
Savage Land
Incident at Ryker's Creek
Death on High Mesa
Wassala Valley Shootout
Marshal of Gunsight
A Killing at Tonto Springs
Lawless Range
Showdown at Crazy Man Creek
Trail to Nemesis
Stopover at Rever
Warpath
Mankiller
Death Trail
Sixgun Predator
The Hanging Man
Last Texas Gun
Meet at Ipona Basin
Return to Callyville
Bushwhack at Wolf Valley
Welcome to Hell
Scallon's Law
Retribution Day
Guntalk at Catalee
Wolf
Hot Day at Noon
Hard-Dying Man
Killer on the Loose
Blood on the Sky
Death Range
Big Trouble at Flat Rock
Scar County Showdown

Six for Texas

Elliot Long

ROBERT HALE · LONDON

First published in Great Britain 2013

ISBN 978-0-7198-0670-4

Robert Hale Limited
Clerkenwell House
Clerkenwell Green
London EC1R 0HT

www.halebooks.com

Typeset by
Derek Doyle & Associates, Shaw Heath
Printed and bound in Great Britain by
CPI Antony Rowe, Chippenham and Eastbourne

For
Neil Jones and Vera Cooper
Thank you for the music

CHAPTER ONE

Clearwater Valley, Colorado, 2 July 1865.

Roughly three months had gone by since Robert E. Lee and Ulysses S. Grant sat down to sign the peace accords at Appomattox Courthouse. But the most damnable thing was, only five days later John Wilkes Booth shot Abraham Lincoln to death in Ford's Theatre, Washington, thus depriving that great president of the chance to begin to build the peace after a war so bitterly fought and won. Even so, thought Tom Nation, they got that no good son of a bitch Booth; by God, they got him!

Now he, his son Frank, Clay Nash and Ed Colerich pulled rein on this high point of the East Ridge. Basking in the warm sunshine of this early afternoon, Tom looked down at the place where the T Bar N once stood. What greeted his gaze caused his face to set into bitter lines.

The outbuildings – bunkhouse, barns, sheds, corrals – as well as the ranch house, were in ruins. Just aged, charred stumps and scattered grey ashes, most of which had long since been blown away by the stiff breezes that, from time to time, blew down this ten miles wide, forty miles long basin between the pine-clad hills. Only the field stone chimney remained erect, pointing like an accusing finger at the sky.

His 22-year-old son, Frank, sitting his trail-worn roan next to him hitched uneasily in the saddle, turned his blue-grey gaze off the scene of dereliction below and said, 'We could've expected better, Pa.'

Tom nodded. 'That's for damned sure, son.'

Tom let his brooding gaze once more drift across the ruins below and then on, up the long, peaceful valley. Not only were the ranch buildings burnt to the ground, there was no sign of their mixed herd of longhorns and Herefords – last count, before they left the valley to fight that damned war near two thousand head. A man could only speculate but to Tom's way of thinking it stood to reason that both Confederate and Union forces, as well as Indians, must have passed through this valley one time or another during those four years of hell just gone. Unattended beeves must have been a real tempting sight. Top of that, Long Riders must have taken their share of prime steers over the years, damn their thieving hides!

Looking at the destruction now, Tom accepted what a fool he had been. But at the time he had been so filled with patriotic fervour when the news of the attack on Fort Sumter broke and a state of war existed between the North and South, that it had completely scrambled his usually sound thinking. Not only that, his long-standing enthusiasm for the emancipation of the blacks, and his intention to join the Union forces, should the call ever come, had also infected his crew – as well as his son, Frank, then only eighteen years old.

In fact, Tom's zeal had been so powerful that the entire

complement of hands on the T Bar N, with the exception of Joseph Brooks, native of Tennessee, had raised long-held 'Yeeee-haaaahs!' when he told them of his intention to ride to Denver to sign up as soon as he had got things straightened out here. Indeed, it was only Joseph Brooks who figured the South was right and that it was no damned business of the North what the Confederation of Southern States did with their black folk, and in their own back yard as well, Goddamnit! However, despite Joseph's preferred politics, all the boys wished him well as the following day, Joseph mounted up and rode East, turning only once to give them a wave and a long, sad look.

Tom then remembered the frenzy of activity that followed his decision to enlist. They turned out the milk cows, the pigs, the hens and the rest of the remuda after picking out the best horses for personal use.

After that they secured the place as best they could. Then they rode to the settlement of Three Forks, under the western foothills at the head of the Clearwater, to tell the mayor their intentions, though Tom never quite knew why he felt he needed to do that.

In any case, he was briskly rebuffed when he did. Josh White, General Store owner and elected mayor of Three Forks stared at him with incredulity before asking what the devil he expected *him* to do about it? Go live out there on the T Bar N until they came home again?

'Not a chance in hell,' announced Josh finishing with, 'you gone plumb crazy, Tom, leaving your place wide open to any Tom, Dick or Harry that's passing by?'

Taken by surprise by Josh's lack of enthusiasm for the coming conflict and his own personal readiness to take a full part in it, Tom stared for moments at the disgruntled mayor. Then he raised his thick eyebrows. 'As you wish, Josh,' he said. 'I guess every man knows his own mind.'

'Indeed he does,' Josh briskly said, 'or should.'

However, it was with a feeling of intense disgust that Tom turned his horse and, with the boys, rode the eighty miles to Denver to enlist.

Dropping his thoughts again, Tom stared up the valley. With hindsight, maybe Josh had been right. Perhaps it had been a crazy thing for Tom Nation to do, leave the ranch he had worked his ass off to build up for nigh on twenty years to the will of God and anybody else who happened to be passing by. But, dammit, he had not expected the war to drag on four years. In fact, he had expected the conflict to last no more than three months and for he and the boys to have been back on the T Bar N in no time at all.

Tom narrowed his eyelids. Well, sure as hell, he had got that one wrong. Those Southern boys proved to be the most tenacious of fighters, never knowing when to quit. And despite peace being declared, in some places a lot of those guys were still fighting that damned war, or so rumour had it.

Tom fiddled with the reins on his horse now. And that was not the worst of it; out of the five riders that left the T Bar N with him and Frank, only two now survived – Ed Colerich and Clay Nash. And right now, they were sitting their horses by his side on this craggy East Ridge looking, with clear and perhaps even bitter disappointment, at the dereliction below.

Tom heaved a great sigh. Well, no use thinking on it. What was done was done and a man could not change that.

However, he did wonder how Brad Killeen of the Circle K, fifteen miles up the valley and his best neighbour, had fared. Brad and his four boys had also announced their intention to enlist when a state of war was declared. And, like him, they also thought the conflict would last no more than three months, six at the most, and had accompanied Tom and his boys on the ride to Denver. But Tom now had to concede that Brad had acted with more prudence than he had done. Brad left three oldsters, his wife Colette and daughter Amy to look after things while he and his boys were gone. Tom Nation had left no one, and that was why he could only damn himself for a fool now.

He turned to Frank. 'Seems we've got some rebuilding to do, son.'

Frank raised blond brows. 'You can say that again. But that'll take money, Pa. And right now' – he waved a big hand at the empty valley below – 'I'd say we're plumb cleaned out.'

'Not quite,' Tom smiled. 'Fortunately, I did something right before we left to fight that damned war. Our nest egg is still resting in that Denver bank accruing interest. John Millard, the manager and an old friend, as you know, informed me by letter only six months ago of what we had in our account. It's a pretty handsome sum.'

Frank's look became a little happier and he said, 'Well, that's something, I guess.' Then he frowned. 'But, dammit, Pa, you could've let me know about the money in case you got yourself killed.'

'I could have, I guess,' admitted Tom. But then he grinned. 'But look on the bright side, son; at least nobody's tried to squat the place while we've been gone.

Now, that's got to be worth something, ain't it?'

Frank said, fiercely, his lean features sullen, 'Somehow, I wished to God they had. It'd maybe help me get rid of some of the meanness I got inside me these days.'

Hearing that, Tom held his gaze on his son's lean, bitter features – a face made old beyond its years by what the boy had been called upon to do during those four years of hell just gone. Frank stared down the valley. He fondled his belt gun, a .36 Colt Army cap-and-ball six-shooter. In addition, he carried three wounds because of that damned war; a sabre slash across the shoulders and two bullet holes; one in his right thigh that left him with a slight limp and one in his left side that had been very slow to heal. And all of the wounds gave Frank trouble when the weather changed. But the most damnable thing was that at one time Frank had been the life and soul of Clearwater Valley; the prankster, the one to liven up a dull hoedown, the fellow with the big grin, the one with blonde hair and the twinkling blue-grey eyes; the one that all the girls made eyes at before Amy Killeen of the Circle K claimed his full attentions. Now Frank was this brooding, watchful man who seldom joked or skylarked around and it was with clear purpose he carried that .36 Colt Army pistol, holstered on his right hip. Not only did he carry that belt weapon; there was the Henry repeater nestled in the soaped saddle scabbard front of his right leg. That, Tom knew, had also done serious harm to more than one Johnny Reb these past four years. And further to those deadly shooting irons, Frank was also armed with a Reb Le Matt, a weapon he took off the body of the Confederate lieutenant he'd killed during fierce hand-to-hand fighting at Yellow Tavern, the place where that Reb Major General J.E.B. Stewart finally got himself sent to glory.

When the story was told, Tom now recalled, that the clash with the Reb lieutenant had been a murderous confrontation and had earned Frank a real fighting reputation in the regiment. Armed only with his Bowie knife, his Colt and rifle being empty, Frank, instead of backing off, stepped in close as the Reb officer came rushing at him with his sabre raised above his head.

Ducking under the swinging blade, Frank had closed in and rammed his Bowie into the lieutenant's wide-open gut, ripping him from navel to breastbone. Regardless, the Reb, even though blood was gushing from his gut and mouth and he was staggering like a drunken man, did manage to back-swing his blade. But the shock of the wound must have taken most of the power out of his strike so the slash Frank received across his shoulders proved minor. However, everybody agreed, the prize was the Le Matt. Rumour had it that it was a deadly weapon at close quarters and its set-up was unique. Immediately beneath the main barrel sat the short 18-gauge shotgun barrel on which the cylinder revolved. When the nine loads in the cylinder had been expended, an adjustment of the hammer would bring the scatter load to bear. Tom narrowed his eyelids at the recollection. And right now he knew that that armament was tucked into Frank's deep inside coat pocket and primed for instant use. And not only were there those deadly weapons in Frank's armoury, there was still the long-bladed Bowie knife he kept sheathed and tucked into his right boot top – the very knife he opened up the Reb lieutenant with. So, with that deadly reputation established, the commander of their division soon had Frank making long, lone sorties behind enemy lines to gather information regarding Reb troop movements.

Tom shook his head at that one. Man, it had taken real guts to do that job. But he now bit his lower lip and felt no small regret at having got the boy into that hell in the first place. He reckoned that was why there was so little merriment to be found in Frank's blue-grey eyes now, only hard-edged warning. And he accepted it would take a whole lot of normal living to get Frank back to being the easy-going fellow he once was. Perhaps that never would happen, and that was a real sadness. But maybe if he. . . .

Tom cleared his throat and eyed his son. He said, 'How are things with you and Amy Killeen these days, boy? If I remember aright, you were real sweet on that gal and she on you – writing to each other and all.'

Tom saw what he thought was a pang of guilt – or was it shame? – pass across Frank's lean, hard features and moments of what Tom construed to be hesitant thought passed before Frank said, 'After a while I never answered her letters; I thought it better if I didn't.' Frank's stare now challenged. 'Dammit, Pa, I could've got killed any time, you know that.'

'But?' Tom prompted.

Frank glared at him, clearly uncomfortable with the discussion. However, he said, 'But she kept on writing to *me*. Now I feel sorry as hell about stopping and I just don't know what she'll think of me when we meet up again.'

Tom sighed. 'Well, what's done can't be undone, son. But from what I know, some women can be real tenacious when they get to love a man real hard. And right now I got the feeling Amy Killeen is still up there on the Circle K, waiting for you to come back to her.'

Tom was not surprised to see something akin to bright hope come to Frank's troubled face when he mentioned that possibility. 'D'you reckon, Pa?' he said, his gaze searching. 'Gee, I've been thinking that maybe I'd be the last person she'd want to see after what I done; that maybe she's even got a new man now and a couple of kids to look after.'

Tom pursed his lips. 'It's possible, I guess, and it's something you'll have to find out. However' – he paused to waved a hand at the ruins of the T Bar N below – 'right now we've got to make plans regarding the ranch. *We got to rebuild, boy.*'

Frank narrowed his eyelids. He well knew his father's habit of playing his cards close to his chest, a damn stupid habit in his opinion, his one son being the only close family he had apart from his great friend Ed Colerich, who, right now, was sitting his horse next to his pa. Frank stared at his father, deep suspicion in the look. 'You been cooking something up while we've been sat here?'

Tom's look of amazement was as near to a newborn's innocence as it was possible to be. He cleared his throat before he spoke. 'Somebody's got to do it, boy, and, yes, I have been turning a few things over, can't deny. You know me, son, always looking to the future.'

'Yeah, I know,' Frank said cynically, 'so spill it.'

Tom cleared his throat once more. 'Well, right now we need to rebuild, like I mentioned just now.'

'Goes without saying,' Frank said, glaring.

'Then we've got to restock.'

Frank nodded impatiently. 'Again, it don't need to be

said.' Once more he narrowed his eyelids to indicate his distrust. 'You've got a plan, ain't you? Go on, admit it.'

Tom straightened up in the saddle. 'Well, I never could fool you for long, could I, boy? All right, I have and here it is: I leave you to deal with the rebuild here while I head for Texas to buy the nucleus of a new herd. It seems to me it's the logical thing to do.'

Frank stared his incredulity. 'Are you being serious, Pa?' he said. 'From what I hear Texas is a mighty dangerous place right now. It's full of Johnny Rebs with chips on their shoulders the size of logs. If it's got to be anybody that goes there, dammit, it's got to be me, being the younger, fitter man and the future boss of the T Bar N.'

Tom nodded his head with apparent enthusiasm now. 'And normally I would agree, but d'you reckon you'll be able to hold down that temper of yours long enough when you come into contact with Johnny Reb again, after what you've been through? I reckon it'll take the sort of tact you once had but don't have any more.'

'I'll handle it,' Frank said. 'I'm a man grown now.'

Tom said proudly, 'That you are, son, no denying, and that's why I reckon you're the fellow to handle the hefty chore I'm offering you here.' He now raised his big hands, palms up in urgent appeal. 'Can't you see it, son? It'll need young men, not the likes of me, to head for those hills to swing those axes and tow those pine trunks down into the valley in order to rebuild. Think on it, boy,' he implored, 'that house and all that goes with it will be yours one day. Now, you don't want some old mossy horn like me to design it for you, do you? And I'm sure Amy Killeen, or any other gal you end hitching up with, will have more than a smidgen to say about that if I even begin to try.'

Frank stared long and hard at his father. 'Got it all figured out, ain't you, old man?' he said. 'Well, maybe I'm not fixing to marry right now – you thought of that? And you sure know how to use the words. Allus been good at that, ain't you? Allus been able to twist men around your little finger.'

Tom gave Frank his hurt look. 'Just using my head, son. You've got to admit, the plan is the sensible way to go about it.'

Frank scowled. 'Meaning I haven't got no sense when it comes to figuring things out? That what you mean?'

Tom frowned before he said, 'Now you're being stupid, boy. You know better than that. You know I have nought but the highest regard for you. You're a son any father would be proud of. I'm just trying to be practical, that's all. Gosh darn it, all I want is for you to be settled and happy with a woman in that house you're going to build. And, dammit, I want grandchildren to bounce on my knee and generally spoil in my old age. Now, that ain't much for a man to ask, is it?'

'Just can't wait to get me up that aisle, can you?' said Frank.

'Dammit, that's rich!' replied Tom. 'One time you couldn't get enough of Amy Killeen. What's changed you, boy?'

Frank's look was bitter. 'That damned war, is what.'

Tom wafted a dismissive hand. 'Aw,' he said, 'you'll alter when you clap eyes on her again. I'd bet my boots on it.'

Frank stared down at his father's badly worn saddle boots with some disgust before he looked up and said, 'Are you out of your mind, old man? Dammit, those boots ain't worth betting a dime on!'

Sitting their horses close by, Ed Colerich guffawed loudly and Clay Nash roared with laughter. Tom also managed to raise a smile at his son's humour, even though it wasn't clear if Frank meant to amuse.

Indeed, Frank was looking moodily down into the valley and Tom thought he could read his son's thoughts, his present demeanour was so transparent. Like maybe he would be thinking his old mossy horn of a father was as wily as a mesa full of coyotes. And maybe he was thinking, dammit, he never had been able to best the old coot in an argument. And, once more the older Nation's reasoning had come out right, that it had to be Tom Nation that went to Texas, because Frank Nation did not know how he would react when he bumped into Johnny Reb again. Even so, Tom was surprised when his son said:

'OK, you win; when do we get started?'

'I reckon we're already on the trail, boy,' Tom said fondly. He turned to Clay Nash and Ed Colerich. 'How d'you figure it, boys?'

Ed Colerich pursed his lips. 'I reckon you've got it about right, Tom.' Then he added, 'I'd like to ride along with you, if I may.' He turned to Frank. 'But that's no reflection on your abilities, boy.'

Frank growled, 'I know that.'

'Texas for me, too, boss,' Clay Nash said.

Tom nodded and grinned. 'Just like I've been figuring all along. Old heads win out every time.'

Frank greeted that one with a disgruntled growl. Couldn't be too soon for him if it would get these old cusses out of his hair!

CHAPTER TWO

Tom Nation shovelled another forkful of beans and fatback bacon into his mouth as he resumed the recollections of that day of decision two months ago. Things had sure gone along apace since then. Within a fortnight all the plans he had proposed had had their rough edges smoothed out and he'd drawn money out of the Denver bank. With the cash in his pocket – the rest left in the bank for Frank to use when needed – he, Ed Colerich, Clay Nash and a youth by the name of River Tolland had headed for Texas.

He had taken the 16-year-old boy along because Jenny Tolland, the boy's mother and an old friend, had begged him so to do. However, he had been reluctant at first to accommodate the lad because it was well known he was a trifle slow. But, as Jenny explained, pleaded almost, she was desperate for the boy to acquire a trade of some sort so he would be able to make his own way through life when she was gone. But the thing that finally swung it for Tom was the knowledge that Jenny had lost her husband Jacob at Gettysburg. Jacob had also been a good friend and that had made the request all the easier to agree to, even though he did need experienced men for the journey he was about to undertake. However, upon talking to the lad, he found there was something about him that intrigued him, enough to cause him to go against his better judgement and take him on.

And he soon discovered he need not have worried. On the way down here River had quickly proved his worth. And another bonus was that the boy seemed to have a way with horses. He handled the small remuda real well, hardly needing to raise his voice to get them to do what he wanted. And they always seemed to calm down when he was around. Even so, Tom had to accept River was not yet in the category of a top hand but the boy was fast getting that way.

So here he was with the boys, camped by the side of this pleasant river fifty miles into the Texas Panhandle. And because of that it was with some satisfaction regarding his judgement of men that he now allowed his gaze to go beyond this tree-lined stream to the grassy slopes where his five hundred head of cattle were contentedly grazing.

So far he and the boys had met with little trouble and it was pleasing to know that on the morrow they would be rounding up those beeves and heading them out toward the Clearwater and hopefully the rebuilt T Bar N ranch. He also held high hopes that a little lady by the name of Amy Killeen would be there to adorn that new build.

Smiling at that pleasant thought, Tom now reviewed the other man eating with him by the camp-fire. Clay Nash, he accepted, was one of his best men. Clay had been with him for all of eighteen years, had fought that damned war alongside him. Clay had real pedigree. He was third generation frontier stock, as hard as nails and would take nothing from any man. As for Ed Colerich, well he was his life-long friend and right-hand man, indeed, a brother in all but blood. And right now, having eaten earlier, Ed was out on the range, riding nanny on the herd. It was typical of the man, putting the ranch and his best friend's affairs first.

Fond memories as well as the sad ones now came as he brought Ed to mind. Ed was the one that came West with him. Ed was the person that helped him build the T Bar N ranch house and outbuildings, settle the Clearwater Valley, build up the T Bar N herd, fight off the Indians, clear out the buffalo and do battle with any thieving Long Riders that happened to be passing their way. *Ed was also the man that saved Tom Nation from himself.*

But there were good times as well as bad. In particular, 10 April 1841, the day Tom Nation married Mary Woodall, with Ed Colerich acting as best man, in the small wooden church the citizens of the West Virginia town of Oak Lee built using monies collected through public subscription. Oak Lee being the town he, Mary and Ed had been born and brought up in.

Soaking up the memories, Tom stared into the distance. God, what plans he and Mary had had, and how keen had they been to put them into operation. Within a week of being married they had loaded their wagon, said their goodbyes and headed West, the whole town turning out to see them off. However, the real surprise came when, only ten miles into the journey, Ed rode up with that easy smile on his face and said, 'Like to ride along, Tom, if I may.'

Now some might think that was a strange thing for Ed Colerich to do and for Mary and Tom Nation to allow him to, fit young man like Ed with the world at his feet. So Tom thought it was reasonable to ask why Ed needed to make that request. 'You've got to have good cause, Ed,' he said.

Ed shrugged. 'Thought real hard about it while I watched you drive off up the trail. Never did mention I've been figuring on going West myself, so it came to me right then, why not make the ride with two of the best friends a man is ever likely to have. Maybe I can even help you settle in before I move on.'

Tom gazed wistfully into the big arc of blue Texas sky above this pleasant tree-lined stream. That was twenty-four years ago and Ed was still with him, still working his ass off for the T Bar N. And the reason for that was down to one terrible event: the death of Mary, his wife.

11 November 1843 it was. Ed was making the trip with the flat wagon to the Mexican settlement of Percepción, thirty miles to the southwest of the Clearwater, the village where they had gotten all their supplies since arriving in the valley.

They needed to stock up for winter. There had already been one big snow and after seeing the increasing number of wild animals coming down from the mountains, Ed had reckoned there would be another big fall on the way and winter, with all its Colorado fury, was on the verge of piling in on them.

And there had been other anxieties on that fated day, too, Tom recalled. Judging from earlier runs, Ed should have been back the previous day. However, the weather had been inclement from the start – rain and sleet, almost continuously. God only knew what weather Ed was running into on the journey back through the mountains.

Yeah, *11 November 1843.*

The date was seared into his memory.

Tom swallowed on the lump that had now grown large in his throat. Even after all these years he still woke up in the night sweating and hearing Mary's pitiful cries. He could still see the blood flowing from her as he delivered the baby Frank. He could still see her big, round blue eyes staring up at him, anguish locked deeply into them, pleading for him to do something.

He tried everything he knew to stop the bleeding. But in the guttering light of the two candles and the wind howling like a demented soul around the stout, caulked timber walls of the ranch house, the only thing he could do after all his efforts was to hold her clamped to his breast and cry as she slowly slipped away from him.

He had never felt so alone as he did that night, or so angry or so utterly helpless. And this entire thing going on while his newborn son lay bloody and bawling in the cot he and Ed had made for the infant not three months before, and in which he had placed the child while he fought to save Mary's life.

In his desperation, he had even called upon the Lord to intervene. But the Lord chose not to hear him that day. Instead, He left him to watch as his wife of barely two and a half years died before his stricken gaze.

Then came the recriminations. To his mind, in that moment of intense anguish, there was only one person to blame for Mary Nation's death and that was Tom Nation. If he hadn't made Mary pregnant she would still be alive today. But the bald truth was she wanted children – craved them, in fact. Indeed, she often declared she would not feel fulfilled as a woman until she did have children, a whole passel of them. So how in all the world could he deny her that natural desire? Dammit, he'd wanted children, too!

But at the moment of her death he felt as though he had been ripped apart, emotionally as well as physically. And as the night closed in all he could do was sit with her in his arms and stare at the new Colt Paterson cap-and-ball five-shot he had brought West with him, along with his half-stock Sam Hawken rifle.

Yes, there it was, that Colt Paterson resting invitingly on the crude sideboard he and Ed had made early in the spring. He'd thought all he needed to do was get up, walk over, pick up the revolver, place the barrel end against his temple and pull the trigger and Mary and he would be together forever. He even recalled, in his despair, his own desperate urge to just get up and do it. But he held back and stared and cried out in his utter misery.

Ed Colerich arrived back the following day, head bowed into the teeth of a roaring blizzard. Near exhausted, he guided the equally tired horse into the relative warmth of the barn. He took the game animal out of the shafts, stalled it, groomed it and gave it water and grain and filled the hayrack with feed. Then he went out. Closing the swing doors firmly behind him, he once more leaned into the blizzard and made his way to the ranch house, which was now barely visible in the near whiteout. As he drew near, the place looked deserted, not a light showing anywhere. And as he got closer he could hear the faint sounds of a baby crying. But it was not only the cry of a *hungry* infant; it was also the bawl of a child suffering other distresses. Ed knew because he had four sisters who were all married with children. All manner of infant noises were a commonplace to him and had been an everyday part of his life until he rode West with Tom and Mary.

So what the hell had happened here?

Uneasy now, Ed drew his Colt Paterson five-shot – he and Tom had bought one apiece before they came out here – from under the warm protection of his buffalo-skin coat. The worst setting he could imagine was Indians. Rumour had it the Comanche and Kiowa were active in the area. If they were, they would likely have done what they came to do and would be long gone now. For he knew those murderous heathen did not hang around after they had done their deadly work. But it was odd they had not fired the place.

Grim-faced, Ed cocked his five-shooter and entered the ranch house.

In the dimness of the interior he swung his Colt in a half circle, prepared to fire. But what met his gaze stunned him. Nevertheless, he quickly regained his composure, closed the door against the howling wind and flurrying snow and latched it. Then he stood and stared at the scene and circumstances that greeted him. First, the room was bitterly cold. Both candles and the fire were out. The only light there was filtered in through the pieces of scraped calf hide that were nailed against the two squares left to make into windows when glass became available. Even the wooden shutters weren't closed against the storm.

The baby was screaming its head off in the cot. Tom was

kneeling by the bed Mary and he had brought with them from Oak Lee. But what alarmed Ed most of all was the Colt Paterson cap-and-ball five-shot gripped tightly in Tom's big, calloused right hand. Thankfully, as far as Ed could make out, it had not been fired. Tom's free left hand, Ed now observed, was holding his wife's lifeless right one. Tom appeared to be in the grip of some appalling nightmare.

God almighty!

As quietly as possible, Ed peeled off his heavy winter coat, for seeing the bloody bed Mary was lying on and the equally bloody baby in the cot – though the blood on the infant had now congealed – he quickly grasped what had happened: death during childbirth, had to be. And seeing it brought back other tragic memories. Back home in Oak Lee he had stood by ready to help in whatever way he could while one of his sisters died in similar circumstances, despite having the presence of a doctor on that occasion. Oh God! Poor Tom, poor Mary.

But his surge of bitter sympathy did not last long. He quickly pulled himself together and relieved Tom of his gun. His friend did not move; did not appear to realize he was there even; his shocked stare remained fixed upon his wife's face, pallid in death. But the odd thing was, to Ed's present state of mind anyway, Mary seemed to have been serenely peaceful at the moment of her death.

But this was no time for speculation. Ed wrapped the baby in a woollen blanket, and then he built and lit a fire, and put a kettle of snow on to boil. After that, he washed the bawling baby and fed it cow's milk, warmed by that same fire. Next, he winded the infant and wrapped him in clean linen and changed the bed sheets. Then, with the gentle rocking of his arms, the exhausted boy fell asleep. That need now achieved, Ed gently laid the infant back in the cot and placed the clean woollen blanket over him. Even so, Ed knew he wasn't through. Now he eased Tom away from Mary and took his old friend in his arms and hugged him while trying to absorb some of the anguish that must be raging in his mind. And Tom seemed to know he was there and that he was holding him and talking to him. However, Tom continued to stare at Mary while saying over and over that he had killed her and wanted to die with her and to leave him alone. But Ed figured that was not like Tom Nation at all and they must be the rantings of a terribly stricken man. Nevertheless, whatever they were, the words were dangerous in his book and he determined Tom would need to be watched closely – for a while anyway. Finally, his old friend drifted into a deep sleep and he laid him down to rest on the dry, beaten earth floor of the cabin, close to the blazing fire.

Then he looked around him as he pondered on what next to do. The answer was not long coming. He hid away Tom's half-stocked Sam Hawken rifle, his Colt Paterson five-shot and what powder and shot were needed to arm them. What knives that were in the house, used for butchering and other things, he also cached. Also sharp tools and cutlery and ropes capable of bearing a man's weight, he concealed those as well. He could not take any chances with Tom in his present frame of mind.

After those precautions he wrapped the dead Mary in a sheet and carried her out into the raging blizzard. Using the length of rope he'd brought with him he hoisted her into the big cottonwood close to the bunkhouse. He did not want the wolves or coyotes to get to her while he waited for the thaw to come so he could dig a hole deep enough to bury her. For right now, the ground was frozen hard as rock and was nigh impossible to excavate.

The chance to bury her came two weeks later, when an unexpected thaw set in. But by now Tom was just a shuffling apology for the man he had once been and was of little help with anything. But his friend would return, Ed determined, and be his *compadre* once again.

Ed dug Mary's grave on the top of the hill Tom had designated to be the family burial ground when they first arrived. He laid Mary gently in it and placed a cross with her name, date of her birth and date of death carved on the crossbar. Then, reading from the King James version of the Bible Mary had brought with her on their journey West, and with Tom standing sobbing quietly by his side, Ed recited a prayer for the dead over her. After that he stood staring at the cold mound of earth and allowed his own tears to fall.

The days slid by. Still there was no improvement in Tom. But that did not put Ed out, for the day would surely come when Tom would be returning to his old self again and the real healing could begin in earnest.

Meanwhile, he did the necessary chores around the ranch as well as feeding, cleaning, bedding and comforting the infant Frank when needed. And in between those times he talked to Tom, listing all the things his best friend had to live for: the boy, the T Bar N, the big plans he and Mary had had for the ranch. 'Think hard on that, Tom,' he said, 'if not for you, for her.'

But Tom did not to want to hear. He was waiting for the moment when Ed dropped his guard. Inevitably, the chance came. Mid-December it was; the 14th to be exact. Above the noise of the blizzard howling outside he could hear Ed busy in the kitchen, clattering and whistling and preparing a supper of antelope stew and cow's milk for the boy.

During this period of being alone Tom felt an urge to be secretive. Being so calm now, Ed was probably thinking his old friend Tom Nation was over the worst and he could relax a little. Not so, old pal, Tom thought. There is nothing left for me here. You, old friend, can have the ranch, with my blessing. I've even put it in writing so there will be no doubts when I'm gone.

With those thoughts Tom fondled his Colt Paterson, which was hidden in his deep coat pocket. Days ago, he had found out where Ed had hidden the weapon and once he had discovered where the powder and shot was he had loaded it.

A strange fascination now filled him. All he needed to do now was put the barrel to his temple and press the trigger and he would be with Mary. But shocking him to the very roots of his being was what seemed to be Mary's voice coming at him from out of nowhere – strong and sharp and full of anger. '*Don't you even think about it, Tom Nation! You have a boy to rear, our boy! See you get it done, Goddamnit!*'

Astonished by that strident command, for Mary never blasphemed, he looked around the big room. Nothing, just the candlelight casting weird shadows on the walls and roof, the roar of the wind outside, the gurgles of baby Frank awakening, the hiss of snow beating against the stout door and walls and the crackle of the logs on the fire.

Stunned, he slowly lowered his gun. He hardly heard Ed come in from the kitchen carrying the baby's warm milk. He barely heard him put the milk down and he did not resist when his friend took the big Colt Paterson out of his hand before saying, 'Thought twice about it, huh, old buddy?'

Tom looked at his friend, still dumbfounded. 'Mary came to me, Ed,' he said, his astonishment still evident. 'She spoke to me.'

Ed said, 'She did, huh?' Then with the deft fingers of a man knowing guns he eased the loaded cylinder out of the Colt and rendered it useless. After that he said, 'What she have to say?'

'That I've got to live and rear the boy.'

Ed nodded as if he had had something confirmed. 'Well, I allus did say she had more sense than the two of us put together.'

Tom looked at him as if seeing him for the first time in weeks. He said, 'Yeah, you allus did say that, didn't you, old friend?'

Ed laid the disarmed gun on the table and then made to pick up the bottle to feed the baby Frank, but Tom put a hand on the bottle and said, 'Reckon that'll be my job from now on.'

For the first time in weeks, Ed grinned. 'Yeah,' he said, 'I guess it will at that.'

Then he went into the kitchen, carrying the disarmed Paterson. Once more came the clatter of dishes and the whistling, but the whistling had more spirit to it now and the antelope stew smelled just like heaven to Tom.

CHAPTER THREE

However, Tom never did hear Mary's voice again. Even though he took flowers to her grave on the hill above the ranch every week and talked to her for a full hour or more, there was no reply, just the rustle of the breeze through the sweet-smelling grass and flowers and the song of the birds trilling on the wing.

Occasionally, he had the fanciful idea that those sounds and smells were the *presence* of Mary and that she was with him and talking to him. Maybe it was crazy for a man to think that way, but he did. And somehow, over the years, that whimsical idea gave him peace and, indeed, contentment.

Once more he looked at the Texas sky, this time with a wistful gaze, and then let the memories slip away. That was twenty-two years ago and this was now. He gazed at the gently flowing stream, gliding through this shallow valley they were camped in. Unsurprisingly, to him, he realized that tears were rolling down his granite-like features and that the boys were giving him looks.

But they knew why he grieved, or at least Clay Nash did

and he suspected the Tolland boy did, too. Word would have been passed around regarding that terrible event in so small a community as that of Clearwater Valley. Even so, they might be wondering why such a strong man as Tom Nation mourned for so long. Well, they'd know if it had happened to them, by God!

Tom wiped his deeply wrinkled eyes with a far from clean handkerchief and with an effort of will pulled himself together. It was time he relieved Ed Colerich while the boys carried out designated chores around the camp.

He got up and washed his enamel plate and cup in the stream, then stowed them away with his other belongings in the trail wagon. Then, from his coat pocket, he lifted out his pipe, along with his tobacco pouch. His briar filled, he returned the tobacco pouch and stared at the herd. His feeling of contentment was complete and his excitement at the prospect of once more building up the T Bar N quietly exhilarating.

It was as he raised his gaze from filling his pipe that he saw the party of riders coming over the crest of the hill about a mile to the west. Though they were still dark specks amongst the clouds of yellow dust they were kicking up, they were growing in size all the time. In what seemed no time at all they were now coming down the long slope into the willows and cottonwoods that lined the stream.

Tom felt his gut inexplicably tighten, his eyelids narrow. For some primal reason his instincts were telling him that this was not a good situation. Even so, he stuck a twig into the dying embers of the cook fire and lit his pipe and puffed on it while he waited for the riders to arrive.

When they got to within a hundred yards of the camp

they eased back on the reins and walked their horses the rest of the way. And, confirming his instincts, Tom soon assessed this was no ordinary bunch of riders. These were mean-looking men and well armed. Some were bearded; most wore parts of tattered Confederate grey uniforms. Others had Reb kepis and battered campaign hats on their shaggy, unshorn and unwashed heads. Ex-Confederates to a man, had to be.

He flicked a glance toward Clay Nash and River Tolland. Clay was also watching the riders come in with guarded interest while forking the last of his beans and bacon into his mouth.

River Tolland, on the other hand, was not eating. His taut, lean, youthful and at times vacant-looking face was, at the moment, showing real concern. And, as was his habit when disturbed by people with whom he was not familiar, he began blinking rapidly while casting nervous glances at Tom and Clay. Tom got the impression the youth was wondering what he and Clay were going to do about the situation.

When the bunch was close enough Tom removed his pipe from his mouth looked up and smiled at the thickset gent sitting atop a big chestnut gelding and riding a little ahead of the main bunch, suggesting he was their leader.

'Howdy,' he said. 'What can we do for you? Fix you some coffee?'

Hell, what else could he say?

Not one in the bunch returned his smile, apart from a slack mouthed, down-chinned, blonde-haired youth with acne. He was leaning forward, grinning an oafish, yellow-toothed grin. He was wearing two handsome ivory-handled

.36 Colt Navy cap-and-ball six-shooters. One was anchored in a worn officer's holster on his right hip, the flap having been cut away to give easier access. The other weapon was pushed into the leather belt around his slim waist. There was also a Spencer .50 carbine jammed into the leather saddle scabbard by his right leg. A big Bowie knife was sheathed and stuck in his right boot top, haft ready to be grasped at a moment's notice. Tom could not help but wonder who had died so that this spotty, grinning brat could carry such an array of hardware.

He returned his gaze and focused it on the man he directed his words at first off. The rider was wearing a border sombrero and what dark hair showed beneath the broad brim was greying at the temples. At a rough guess Tom reckoned he was about forty years of age, five feet nine inches tall and weighed around one hundred and eighty pounds. The set of his shoulders suggested bull strength and his jutting chin was cleft and covered with dark stubble. He also wore a thick black moustache, similar to the kind Mexicans favour and his features were severe and square. What seemed to be a permanent frown creased his broad forehead. Dangling from his hairy right wrist was a plaited leather quirt.

The man's steel-grey eyes gave Tom the impression they were staring right through him while examining every detail along the way. Tom met that probing gaze with equal thoroughness. Finally, the man leaned back, waved a hand towards the herd grazing the slopes behind him.

'You got title to those beeves, mister?'

Tom shrugged. 'Wouldn't be driving them if I hadn't.'

The man's riveting gaze did not alter. He said, 'Well,

I've been looking. They bear the Lazy S brand . . . my brand.'

Tom felt his gut tighten further and he tried to subdue the prickles of anxiety that were now beginning to run up his backbone. He said, his voice expressing calmness he did not feel, 'Friend, I bought those beeves in good faith at Taylor's Ford not a two days ago. Are you Brock Stedman?'

The man's whole demeanour seemed to go on guard: taut, wary, his eyes now flicking like a snake's tongue as they explored every stern groove of Tom's visage. Then he said, 'How come you know my name?'

'Charlie Hibbert, the fellow I bought the beeves off,' Tom said. 'He showed me your bill of sale. He said he purchased the cattle off you three weeks ago. He claimed his intention was to drive them to Sedalia but then he heard the authorities there were not allowing Texas beef in because of the fear of bringing the fever in with them.' Tom paused, looked up with eyes as hard and brittle as those staring down at him. 'So he sold them on to me,' he went on. 'What's more, he gave me paper to prove it was a legitimate deal.'

Tom made for his inside coat pocket to pull out the bill of sale that Charlie Hibbert had supplied him with when the deal was done. There was a flurry of hands; weapons of various sizes and makes appeared as if by magic in grubby mitts and they were all aimed at him.

Tom stared at Stedman. He said, 'What the hell is this?'

The burly ranch-owner smiled, but the grin was hardly friendly. He said, 'Seems y'all need a little education, friend. In this country you learn not to make any fast moves.' He wagged a finger, as if indicating the pocket Tom had been reaching for. 'Now, what you got in there?'

'The bill of sale, dammit.' Tom handed the paper up to Stedman. The rancher bent in the saddle and took it out of his hand. He read it and then screwed it up and threw it on to the moist, hoof-chewed ground. After that he said, 'Two dollars a head and you figure they're straight?'

Tom eyed the bill of sale in the dirt for a moment before looking up, making his anger all too clear by the grim set of his angular features and the flash in his grey eyes. He said, 'That was the price Hibbert was prepared to accept.' He narrowed his eyelids and leaned forward. 'From what I hear, Stedman, a lot of men don't pay anything for beeves in Texas these days, so many mavericks about. They just round them up, put their brand on them and make money out of them.' His look turned accusatory. 'Is that what you're doing?'

The Lazy S owner's face flushed and he crinkled his fleshy eyelids as he looked at Tom, as if in inquiry. 'Y'all getting lippy with me, mister?'

'Take it how you will,' Tom said. 'One thing is for sure, I'm not used to being called a liar and having my bill of sale thrown into the dirt. That ain't friendly, mister, ain't friendly at all. You going to pick it up?'

Stedman leaned back in the saddle as if he was finding it hard to come to terms with Tom's apparent insolence and disregard for the numbers facing him. The Lazy R owner sighed before he said, 'All right, friend, I'll make it plain to you. That bill of sale you waved at me just now isn't worth the paper it's written on. Those beeves you say are yours happen to have been stolen from my ranch not ten days ago. Me and my boys have been chasing them down ever since.' Then Stedman, as if he thought he needed to have the claim doubly confirmed, turned to the men ranked alongside and behind him. 'Ain't that right, boys?'

One or two grinned wolfishly. The acne-chinned, mean-looking little bastard who was lined up alongside him said, with a snigger, 'Yes siree, ten damned days, just like you say, Mr Stedman, sir.'

The Lazy S rancher turned back to Tom, his smile fixed and mirthless. 'So there it is, friend. What have you got to say?'

'Nothing to what I've already said,' Tom replied. 'They're mine. I bought those cattle in good faith.'

'You did, huh?' Stedman's smile faded and his face once more became ugly. 'Well, y'all know what, fella? I reckon you are a damned liar. I figure you did steal those beeves and then made that bill of sale out to yourself to cover your theft.'

Tom tensed as he glared at the arrogant bastard before him. 'By God, mister,' he said, 'you're pushing it.'

Again Stedman's mouth formed its contemptuous sneer. 'I am, huh?' he said. 'Well, not hard enough, seems to me.' Now his features changed to suggest genuine regret. 'Fella,' he said, 'I've got some real bad news for you; in this part of the world we hang cattle thieves.'

Tom realized his mouth had suddenly become dust dry. He stared hard and long at Stedman before he said, 'Man, you can't be serious.'

At that moment Clay Nash came abruptly to his feet, his empty enamel plate and mug still in his left hand. He stared up at Stedman with steely eyes as he spat out a tough piece of bacon rind. He said, his voice more of a growl, 'By God, fella, you're way out of line here. Tom here's telling the truth.'

Stedman lashed out with his leather quirt. A crimson gash ran red down Nash's face. He gasped harshly and staggered back, his left hand opening to drop his cup and plate as he reached up to hold the gaping wound. Already blood was seeping redly through his fingers.

Stedman leaned forward in the saddle, eyes mean. He pointed at Nash with his now bloody quirt. 'I don't remember asking you a damn thing, mister.'

Recovering quickly, Clay glared up. Rage flushed his rugged, tanned face. He said, 'Why, you low-down son of a bitch!'

Ignoring his wound, Clay grabbed for his Army Colt, which should have been in his hip holster. But like Tom he had taken it off and put it in the back of the trail wagon before they ate. They had not been expecting trouble; all they had anticipated was a peaceful meal and a quiet night before they gathered the herd at first light and headed it north for Colorado and the Clearwater. The clicks of various weapons being armed and sighted directly on to him held Clay in a crouched pose. Tom could see he was seething with frustration.

Stedman grinned evilly and leaned forward in the saddle. 'Don't have a gun, huh?' he said. He shook his head and 'tut-tutted'. 'Well, that's a hell of an oversight in this country, mister, I got to say.'

Clearly incensed now to the point of extreme reckless-ness, Clay lunged forward. He reached up to drag

Stedman out of the saddle in order to punch him silly. However, as if anticipating the move, the Lazy S rancher jerked back on the reins and quickly backed up his big chestnut gelding while at the same time pulling out his long-barrelled Colt. And as soon as Clay was close enough Stedman began beating him about the head with the barrel, the steel flashing dull blue in the afternoon sunlight.

After taking several swipes Clay finally sank to his knees. He was clearly dazed and, adding to the blood already made by the quirt slash, fresh crimson was running down his face from the skull wounds he had suffered because of the pistol beating. It soon became clear to Tom that it was only Clay's iron will that was holding him upright, albeit he was on his knees.

Enraged, his hands clenching into fists, Tom glared up. 'Damn you, Stedman, no call for that.'

The Lazy S owner swung his mount around to face him, his features vicious. 'No? You want some of the same?'

Tom hardened his stare. 'You'll pay hell doing it!'

At that moment, River Tolland, now pale-faced and clearly anxious, said, 'I want to go, Mr Nation. Can we go now?'

Hearing that simple plea, the down-cheeked, pimply-faced bastard next to Stedman stared at River and brayed a laugh. He said, 'Shit, what have we here? A damned numb head?'

Ignoring the acne-troubled brat, and despite the bad feelings he was getting in his gut regarding this developing situation, Tom turned and gave young Tolland a reassuring look. He said, 'It's all right, son. I'll deal with it.'

But Pimple-Chin guffawed. 'Like hell you will, mister!'

As if with delight he pulled out one of his ivory-handled .36 Colt Navy revolvers and began firing. Lead immediately started kicking up dirt around River Tolland's worn saddle boots, close enough to splatter them with mud. Clearly bewildered, the boy yelped and began hopping about while looking wild-eyed at Tom. 'Please, Mr Nation,' he said, 'make him stop!'

Tom made a move toward the acne-chinned wonder but the brat turned his Colt and aimed it straight-armed and sighted at Tom's forehead. His grin was gone now. He said, 'Still one left, mister, and you'll get it between the eyes!'

Tom stopped in his tracks. He knew full well the threat would be carried out without a qualm. The war had made killers of many boys like this one. In fact, they appeared to relish the killing process. Some had already gained certain notoriety; Jesse James, for instance, who was once a member of Quantrill's bunch and was now running with the Youngers.

Stedman chuckled indulgently and said, 'Whoa, Kat, easy now; I'll say who gets what and when.'

Kat Malling glared at Stedman, his pimply face working viciously. Nevertheless, he reluctantly complied with the directive. However, it was plain to see he did not like his play being interrupted and that he was not good at taking orders.

Stedman turned his gaze back to Tom. He was still smiling. 'A little high-spirited, that boy; hasn't had much education to speak of.' He raised thick, dark brows and, as if to enlighten Tom further, continued, 'Plenty of gun education, though, and I guess that's all that counts these days, wouldn't you say?'

Tom held the rancher's cold gaze and said, 'Stedman, the liar accusation I'll overlook for now, but the allegation we stole those beeves is about as far from the truth as you can get.'

Stedman cased his Colt, the barrel still red with Clay Nash's blood. 'Is it now?' he said. 'Well, I'm not inclined to believe you, y'hear?'

The rancher's features now turned savagely mean. He swung round in the saddle and waved an arm at the men lined up behind him. 'Get to hanging the thieving sons of bitches!' he barked.

Great anxiety ran through Tom now. 'This'll be murder, Stedman! You can't do it!'

But already nine men were climbing down and advancing towards them. Most were grinning, clearly relishing the lynching to come. And now knowing that neither reason nor compassion was to be had here, Tom desperately looked around for alternatives.

They could maybe make run for the T Bar N remuda across the river, chance getting aboard a horse and hightailing it out of there. Or they could perhaps make an attempt to reach their guns, which were, at present, resting useless in the back of the store wagon. But both ideas, he knew, were crazy and born out of desperation. Top of that, Clay Nash was still kneeling on the ground semi-conscious and clearly in no fit state to participate in anything. The only option left seemed to be to make a fight of it and hope to God something turned up. Tom had heard the Texas Rangers were scattered across the land, probably disbanded, many having fought the Rebel cause and were now a disorganized bunch just waiting to find out what would happen next to the state they loved. As for other law . . . Tom guessed that in these wild parts it was non-existent. Only the laws a man made himself would take precedence here.

In some despair, he turned to young River Tolland. The boy did not own a gun, and from what Tom knew about him, did not know much about defending himself either, particularly the raw primitive fighting this inevitably would grow into. All he could say was, 'Prepare to defend yourself, son,' then watch as consternation spread across the youth's face.

Tom steeled himself and closed his gnarled hands into rock-hard fists. He still hoped for a miracle, a change of heart, Stedman accepting he really was telling the truth. But at bottom he felt that was never likely to happen. Stedman was clearly a vindictive, as well as a single-minded man, with a streak of sadism running mile-wide right through him. He was enjoying this and clearly no amount of pleading was going to change his mind.

But something distracted Tom; he heard a scuffle to his right and turned to see River Tolland running toward the remuda. Anxiety was etched deep into every line of the boy's face as he kept turning to look anxiously over his shoulder to see if he was being chased.

Whooping like devils, three of the advancing men broke away from the pack of nine and began chasing him. Four other riders turned their mounts from the main bunch, their clear intention: to form a barrier between young Tolland and the now restless remuda.

Feeling helpless as well as desperate, Tom turned to see Clay Nash was now back on his feet and a degree of relief ran through him. At least they were going to make a fight of it now, for already Clay was glaring at the oncoming men, his grey eyes burning like coals through the mess of blood-seeping wounds on his brow and face. And his hands were already bunched into gnarled fists. As Tom expected, Nash was not going to go down easy. But only God knew what was in store for poor River Tolland.

As soon as the three men who had assigned themselves to deal with Clay got close enough he began lashing out with his fists. He punched one man to the ground with a haymaking right and then began wrestling with a second while the third man stood eager-eyed, hovering on the periphery of the action, his Colt held ready to lay it across Clay's skull should he come close enough.

Tom, on the other hand, now felt the intense calm he had always known when danger was imminent. He watched the progress of the three men that had picked him out for treatment and waited. When they got near enough he did not hesitate. He moved in, unleashed a swinging right and then a left uppercut. Both blows connected solidly with the nearest man's thick red neck and jutting, unshaven chin.

Yelling his pain the fellow staggered back, clearly dazed. He tripped on a rotten tree branch, which was half buried in the riverside grass. It caused him to stagger and flail his arms wildly in an attempt to keep his balance. He did not succeed. He hit the ground hard and his faded, worn kepi flew off his head to reveal a dirty bald pate.

Tom figured the man was out of it for now and he

swung to meet the other two men ranked against him. One was already near upon him. He tried to evade his assault but all he could do was take the full force of the man's charge as he crashed like a bull, head first into his right side.

But despite the severity of the pain that ripped through his body on impact, Tom managed to grip the man around the shoulders. Fight-fury pumped through him, swamping his pain. He began throwing a series of punches at the bear of a man he was now beginning to battle with. But the fellow seemed to walk through them and grasped him around the waist with his oak-trunk-like arms. They went down, wrestling desperately in the mud for control. Worse, the man's body odour was rank, suggesting he had not bathed in months. Then Tom saw an opening and he head-butted his assailant and had the satisfaction of hearing the cartilage in the man's nose crack under the impact. It was enough to cause the fellow to grunt and loosen his grip. Blood was already streaming from his nostrils and Tom took the advantage, mustering all his strength to throw the man off him.

Now free of the man's stink and weight, he scrambled to his feet. Nevertheless, the fellow recovered quickly and struggled up with him. But Tom was waiting for him and as he came up level he caught him with an immense right that smashed in under his bristled chin. The punch almost lifted the fellow off his feet and he went crashing to the ground, blood spewing out of his mouth in a crimson spray. He was clearly out of it for the moment.

Fight-mad now, Tom looked around for his other attacker, the blood pouring from a cut above his right eye half blinding him. But the next thing he knew was a blow smashing against his left ear. It sent stars blazing across his vision and his senses spinning.

He went sprawling to the ground. Boots began crunching into him from all angles. All he could do was huddle into a foetal position and clasp his hands around his head in the hope of minimizing the damage while he fought to clear the fuzz from his brain so he could take up the fight again. However, he knew deep down that was never going to happen. He was fighting against a dark chasm that was relentlessly beginning to creep in on his consciousness. He was on the point of oblivion when he vaguely heard Stedman's harsh call:

'Easy, boys; save enough for the hanging!'

Then complete darkness closed down.

CHAPTER FOUR

As he recovered, Tom could hear Clay Nash was still battling, way over to his left. Harsh grunts were coming, rasping gasps, raw curses and animal-like snarls. But eventually all went quiet; only the bitter expletives of badly mauled men suggested Clay Nash had given a good account of himself before succumbing to the numbers facing him. Well that was Clay, Tom thought, hard as teak and as tough as the land that made him.

Gradually, Tom's senses began to knit together. He realized blood was seeping from half a dozen cuts to his face and head and that pain was saturating his whole body. Top of that, he could hardly breathe for the agony of what, he was now almost certain, were broken ribs.

As more clarity came Tom looked around him, anxious to find out what had happened to young Tolland. Eventually, his searching gaze found the boy. He was crawling on all fours in the shallows of the river, obviously badly beaten but clearly still striving to get across to the remuda. What heartened Tom most of all, though, was to see that one of River's assailants was sprawled unconscious on the near bank. Even so, his elation was quickly squashed when he observed the other two attackers were splashing after the boy, their intentions very clear.

When they reached him they grabbed him and dragged him back to the bank. Nevertheless, River set to fighting again. But with two brutish opponents now mauling him Tom knew the boy did not stand a chance.

Tom swallowed on his dry throat. He would have had this business end differently or, better still, never to have happened at all. However, he felt a degree of satisfaction well up in him. In the end the boy had shown he had guts when the chips were down. Nevertheless, the guilt came back as he recalled Jenny Tolland's last words to him before they left the Clearwater for Texas: 'You'll take good care of him, won't you, Tom? He's all I have.'

'I'll truly do my best, Jenny,' he had replied. 'You have my solemn word on that.'

He had been so certain he was doing the right thing, giving the boy a chance. Sure the boy had been considered simple. But, by God, he had proved to be competent enough to handle a cowhand's job. In fact he had made plans to keep the boy on at the T Bar N payroll when they got back to the Clearwater he was that good.

But what chance now?

Tom stared up at Stedman through swollen eyelids, ignoring the two men standing over him, ready and waiting to again beat him mercilessly if he made any more bad moves.

'Let the boy go, Stedman,' he said through battered, bleeding lips. 'He doesn't know the time of day. He doesn't even carry a gun.'

Stedman's thick lips curled into a sneer. 'Is that so?

Then y'all should've left him at home.' The Lazy S owner's face now turned vicious as he glared at the men standing over Tom. 'Well, what the hell you waiting for?' he bawled. 'There's the tree. Get the job done, Goddamnit!'

It was then a new voice called out. Refined, Deep South, Tom assessed. He allowed his gaze to seek its author as unreasonable hope rose in him. It was one of Stedman's riders, a young, slightly haughty looking blonde-haired lad wearing a neatly repaired Reb lieutenant's uniform. He was sitting atop a handsome roan mare. Tom reckoned he could be no more than eighteen years of age.

'Major Stedman, suh,' the young man was saying, 'a word, if Ah may.'

Major? Tom found that difficult to believe.

Stedman glared at the young fellow. It was obvious he was fast losing patience with these continued interruptions.

'What now, Goddamnit?'

'Perhaps we should ride into Taylor's Ford, check out this man's story. He and his men seem genuine enough to me.'

Stedman's mean, vicious stare turned steel hard. It seemed to Tom it was a stare that had long ago been stripped of every decent human emotion. 'Y'all reckon, huh?' he said. He cackled a harsh laugh and leaned forward. 'Now, tell me, sonny, how long have you been with the Lazy S?'

'A week, suh; a week Ah must confess Ah am beginning to regret.'

Stedman leaned back as if in mock surprise and looked around at his men. 'Well now, our brave Southern boy is beginning to have re-grets, boys. Maybe he figures our company is not good enough for him.' He turned back to the young Reb. 'W-e-e-ell, *Lieutenant* John Hascot, don't let us keep you from your *re*-grets. As of now you're through with the Lazy S. And, by God, I must have been crazy to take you on in the first place.'

John Hascot's finely chiselled, aristocratic features remained calm as he bowed his head in acquiescence. 'Terms accepted with pleasure, suh. Even so, Ah would still prefer you check their story. If you do not, Ah shall consider you to be no officer of the Confederacy, as you claim to be.'

Stedman stared. Tom saw pure evil was in those eyes now. 'You wouldn't, huh?' he said. 'Well, listen to me, *Lieutenant* John Hascot. I can't do with men questioning my judgement, never could. It doesn't do, see. Above all, I need discipline and for men to keep their mouths shut about my business. So, d'you know what? I've changed my mind; you can get the hell out of here right now, or you get to hang right there with our guests. Am I making things clear to you now, *suh*?'

Stedman's jeer at the Southern 'sir' brought amused leers from the men around him and all were directed toward the youthful officer. Nevertheless, the young man lifted his chin, ignored their stares and gloating looks and continued to gaze steadily at Stedman. 'Very clear, suh,' he said, 'nevertheless, Ah still require to see real justice done, as should you if you are what you say you are.'

Stedman was clearly at the end of his patience. He said, 'You know, I'm getting real tired of you questioning my judgement and, by God, my rank!' He leaned forward. 'So let me acquaint you with a few facts, *Lieutenant.* Right now, I'm the only justice you're ever likely to see in a full two hundred mile radius of here. On top of that, you don't seem to have listened to a damned word I've been saying.' Stedman leaned back. 'Now, I find that real insulting to the boys *and* to me. What is more, you are dangerous. You've got a flapping mouth and there's only one answer to that in my book.'

Stedman pulled his .36 Colt Army cap-and-ball pistol from its holster and shot Hascot twice in the chest. The Reb lieutenant gasped, stared wide-eyed and bewildered for a moment at his slayer before he gave out a sigh and keeled over to drop into the long brown grass, blood pouring out of the two holes left of his sternum. It was clear to Tom the youth had been shot through the heart and was probably dead before he hit the ground.

Raw anger in him, he turned his bleak stare onto Stedman and said, 'By, God, what kind of man are you?'

Stedman's stare latched onto Tom's; an evil smile decorated his lips. 'The kind that requires unreserved discipline, Nation; the kind that can't stand bleeding hearts; the kind that doesn't want useless men around him likely to go telling tales about my business like I suspect our fine, brave lieutenant here was about to do.'

'You're sick in the head,' Tom said.

Stedman grinned evilly. 'No, sir, y'all got that wrong,' he said. 'I'm hale and hearty whereas in a short while you will be *dead.* Now, that's what I call being *real* sick.'

Stedman began to guffaw heartily and Kat Malling stirred beside him – he with the mocking smile, the bad acne on his down-covered chin and the twin, ivory-handled

Colt Navy six-shooters in holster and belt. Grinning, he looked down at the dead Reb officer and said, 'And, by damn, you sure as hell nailed down the lieutenant's coffin, major, sir.'

Stedman turned his Colt. He'd obviously found no humour, even macabre humour, in Malling's jocular remark. He lined his weapon up on the spotty-faced kid. He said, smoothly, even mildly, 'That's very true, Kat. Now, how long have you been with me?'

Malling eyed the Colt pointing right at him before he turned his sky-blue gaze up to meet his boss's stare. 'Four, maybe five years; but, hell you know that.'

The Lazy S owner nodded, slowly. 'That's right,' he said. 'Now, what am I always saying about mouthing off without permission?'

Malling smiled his misleading, lazy smile. Misleading because it had the look of a slavering mountain cat about to strike. There was certainly no humour in it. 'That it ain't good for discipline,' he said. 'But, shit, no harm done right now, huh, boss?'

'That's right,' Brock Stedman said, 'not right now. But because you disobeyed that order, and because you should know better, y'all get to bury the son of a bitch. How y'all feel about that, my young killer friend?'

The look on Malling's face turned to dark menace as his blue eyes paled and took on the colour of glacier ice. He said, 'Well, to hell with that! For one thing, he ain't worth burying!'

Stedman tightened his grip on his Colt and armed it by thumbing back the hammer. He said, 'Even so, you get to do it, boy.'

Despite the deadly menace of Stedman's armed Colt lined up on him, there appeared to be no fear in Kat Malling. After a moment, the baleful look that suddenly appeared on his sallow features faded and that slow grin of his once more formed on his slack lips, exposing his yellow, crooked teeth. Even so, his eyes remained implacably cold and his reply was in no way subservient. If anything, it mocked as he offered Stedman an exaggerated but clearly derisive salute. 'Yes, sir, *Major* Stedman,' he said, 'you're the boss sure enough, allus needing that damned discipline of yours.'

The Lazy S boss nodded slowly. 'So, just remember that, Kat,' he said.

The grin stayed on Malling's lips as he flicked another derisory salute. 'Sure, Major, sir, anything you say.'

But Malling's deathly look never left Stedman's and Stedman knew its portent all too well. But he would deal with that when the time came. He always had done.

CHAPTER FIVE

Stedman now stared at the men holding Tom Nation and his boys. His men had just dragged them to their feet and had brought the boy up from where he lay by the river. No witnesses, Stedman thought, no sweat. But he'd need to have a word with Charley Hibbert. That man could become a liability, giving out Brock Stedman's name like it was confetti.

He stared at his men and pointed. 'OK,' he said, 'now take those sons of bitches to that cottonwood yonder and get it done.'

At the words, Tom's fury once more unleashed itself. Again he began struggling against the hands holding him. 'Damn you, Stedman, enough of this!' But it was obvious his protests were falling on deaf ears. Worse, more blows began to rain down on him and the boys.

Beaten and dazed almost senseless Tom now vaguely realized he was being roughly dragged. He strived to clear his vision. He succeeded only to see River Tolland and Clay Nash being hauled along with him to the nearby stand of riverside cottonwoods.

Once more he struggled and began kicking out, all the while cursing Stedman. The violence of his cussing seemed to affect Stedman, enough for him to bawl, 'Damnation, hang the Yankee bastards! What's the matter with you!'

The harsh demand seemed to have the desired effect. Tom felt another severe blow smack against the side of his head, stunning him. And with renewed vigour hands roughly handled him. Now they were tying his hands behind his back. He seemed to be in a half-world. He was neither conscious nor unconscious, just aware enough to realize hands were now hauling him the final distance to the riverside. Once more he struggled as he felt the roughness of hemp being forced over his head and the noose being jerked tight about his neck.

Then his feet left the good soil and he hung unsupported, his head suddenly exploding into terrible pain, eardrums feeling as though they were about to burst from the pressure the strangling rope was imposing. . . .

When the Yanquis' struggles finally ceased, Stedman spat grey phlegm to the ground and then stared hard at Kat Malling. 'Gutsy bunch,' he said, 'you've got to give them that.'

Malling sniggered. 'Yeah. Gutsy, but *dead.*'

Stedman nodded. 'As you say,' he said. 'Now, bury Hascot, then let's get these beeves moved.'

It was Kat Malling's turn to glare this time and with every grudging spadeful, he grumbled and growled as he interred Lieutenant John Mason Hascot, late of the Confederate forces of the South.

CHAPTER SIX

Tough as teak Ed Colerich, riding nanny on the herd, was a mile and a half north of base camp, on top of a rocky butte at the far end of the T Bar N herd. He was still puzzled by the faint pops of a gun he had heard earlier. The sound had definitely come from the direction of base camp. However, he eventually dismissed it as being Clay Nash showing off his marksmanship by taking a pot shot at some critter or snake.

He felt relaxed and at peace. Things were quiet up here and the herd hardly needed any attention. Only two steers had given him trouble; they had hightailed it behind this butte he was on, probably scared by their own shadows. It happened. For long years Ed had been of the opinion that beeves were generally stupid creatures.

He finally cornered them in an arroyo and chased them back to the herd. Now he was up here enjoying the view, taking tobacco and surveying the gather below. Tomorrow morning he, Tom and the boys would be trailing those beeves north to the Clearwater and home range.

Contentment filled him. He felt sure young Frank

would have got the job of building the new ranch house, bunkhouse and outbuildings done by the time they pushed the herd on to home ground. For, the fact was, the Colorado winter was coming and Ed Colerich wasn't getting any younger, nor was his good friend Tom Nation. He knew through late-night camp-side chats on the way home from that war that Tom was figuring on Frank taking more responsibility around the place when they got back. Also, he knew Tom was hoping Frank would be hitched to some presentable filly so the Nation line could continue when he was gone to meet up with Mary.

The pop of many guns this time abruptly brought Ed out of his pleasant thoughts. He turned his sharp and now troubled blue gaze south. The beeves, all that were near base camp a full mile away, that is, were now beginning to run northwest; clouds of dust billowing above and behind them. And amid those madly running cattle Ed saw riders, lots of them.

He squeezed out the red coal at end of his quirly with callused thumb and finger and dropped the mangled remains to the ground in order to fully concentrate on what was going on to the south. He quickly came to the opinion that it could not be Tom stirring up those critters. That would be a crazy thing to do with the big drive north starting pre-dawn tomorrow.

Now very puzzled, Ed spat. He always reckoned the reflective ejection of spittle at such times usually helped him to think more clearly. And once more it did. Apart from Tom, the only other major possibility causing that run was rustlers, or Kwahadi Comanche, known to be in the area and raising all hell. But how they had got to base camp without being seen God only knew. For sure they had not come past *him* for he would have seen them, unless they came through while he was rousting out those two strays back of the butte. Yeah, that must be the logical reason, he decided. However, whatever the cause, those beasts were running hell-for-leather his way and right now.

The cattle under his immediate care, about a hundred of them spread across this gentle hillside a quarter of a mile below the butte he rested upon, now broke off grazing to begin to stare at the oncoming mass. Those lying chewing cud began to scramble to their feet to join those that had, until now, been standing grazing. Meantime, the roar of hoofs was getting nearer and louder and the beasts close by were becoming ever more restless.

Stampede! Ed felt every fibre and sinew of his wiry body was now on tingling edge. The last thing he wanted right now. But he might as well spit into the wind for, quick as a snap of finger and thumb, the cattle below him began to run, the roar of their hoofs now mingling with the oncoming herd. Soon they merged.

Ed steeled himself to go after them. But one man down there trying to turn that mad, roaring bunch? It would be an act of sheer craziness. And those guns rattling away in the distance and those horsemen coming straight towards him with no sign of pursuit from Tom and the boys … it would be lunacy! All he had was one Remington cap-and-ball six-shooter and a Spencer carbine. But no way did he feel good about his decision.

Now agitated in mind as well as body because of his feelings of impotency, Ed grimly counted fifteen riders weaving in and out of the massive dust cloud the beeves were kicking up down there. He pulled back from the butte's edge, dismounted and bellied up to the ridge so he could more clearly view the run. He quickly came to the opinion they were not Comanche.

The raiders were now turning the herd northwest. As he watched, helpless, Ed could plainly hear their whoops, their howls and the cracking of their bullwhips, as well as hear the popping of their many guns. A feeling of icy coldness settled across his lean stomach. The thing that was bothering him was – what, in the name of God, had happened to his old friend Tom Nation, as well as Clay Nash and the Tolland boy?

If it was the last thing he did, he needed to find out.

CHAPTER SEVEN

A quarter of an hour on, with the stampeding herd hidden in a huge dust cloud in the northwest distance, Ed mounted his roan and rode the mile and a half distance into base camp. What he found there sickened him. The store wagon, the horses, the whole remuda in fact – and the saddles – had been taken, the camp-fire kicked out. However, the most horrific part he found down by the quietly running stream: Tom Nation, River Tolland and Clay Nash hung up and strangled by hemp nooses drawn taut around their necks.

Ed wanted to retch. He could hardly bare to look at the cadavers, their heads lolling awkwardly to one side, purple and swollen and swinging in the still lightly dust-laden breeze drifting in from the big range after the recent wild stampede. In particular, he stared at his life-long friend, Tom Nation.

He said, quietly, 'That's no way for a man to go, old friend, damned if it is.'

Ed continued to gaze at the ghastly scene before he turned his eyes down to read the words spelled out on the grass using polished stones from the river-bed: DEATH TO ALL YANQUI RUSTLERS.

The use of the word 'Yanqui', Ed decided, could only mean one thing: this had to be the work of Johnny Reb, or some of his sympathizers. For, right now, he knew Texas was full of them; men who had bravely fought the Rebel cause and were now trickling home, defeated but by no means broken.

More than likely, they would have no work to return to; many of them would have no homes or families to come back to, either. Ed had also heard that while the men had been away fighting, the Texas Rangers also being in the thick of it, the Kiowa and Comanche had been playing all hell with the settlements. But dammit, they couldn't blame Tom and the boys for that!

Sick at heart, Ed bowed his head and listened to the gentle stream bubbling quietly by. As a salve to his distress he began to remember the many good, as well as the bad, times he had shared with Tom Nation and Clay Nash; the long hours, the hard work, the dedication to the T Bar N. It had been a life lived fully, and, for the most part, happily – the only tragedy being Mary Nation's untimely death. That had happened before Clay Nash's time. Indeed, it had been a grievous blow from which Tom had never fully recovered. And, Ed remembered, he had been pretty badly shaken by the tragic event, too.

After a couple more minutes of silent prayer some instinct was insisting he open his eyes and look up the river-bank. Barely noticeable from where he stood was a mound of freshly dug earth. His curiosity aroused, he remounted his roan and urged it up the gradual slope to level the ground up there. He climbed down and ground-hitched the faithful horse.

Standing staring at the mound of recently turned soil, he looked it over. It was plainly a grave, but there was no board to say who was buried there. To Ed's way of thinking that was a hell of an oversight for any man to make, and it said a lot about the trash he and young Frank, Tom's boy, would have to deal with when they returned to Texas to redress this awful crime. For return they would; Ed had no doubts about that, for, since that damned war, Frank was known to be a very unforgiving man on certain occasions and, by God, that certain occasion did not come any bigger than this.

Ed allowed his gaze to search wider. It wasn't long before he spotted the screwed-up ball of paper lying in the dirt nearby. He picked it up and spread it out, cleaning off the bits of soil that clung to it. It was the bill of sale Charlie Hibbert had laboriously made out in that Taylor's Ford bar, the Blue Star – the only town for a hundred miles around – not three days ago before giving it to Tom as proof of sale.

Ed narrowed his eyelids. It could prove to be useful. He folded the paper and slipped it into one of his vest pockets. After that, he again stared at the mound of earth and decided somebody not known to him must be lying in that ill-prepared grave. It certainly wasn't any of the T Bar N crew, he knew; they were all dead, swinging from that cottonwood down there, God help them.

He decided to dig. There may be items indicating who might be lying there. There might even be details of kin that needed to be informed, even some clue as to who had done this terrible thing. Ed certainly felt it was his bounden duty to notify what relatives there were, should any information come to light. He had done that very thing on more than one occasion during that war – for Rebel and Blue Coat alike.

Now he searched for the base camp spade and pick and soon found them. They had been carelessly thrown aside by somebody after the grave had been crudely dug out and refilled.

He started digging. He found the grave was no more than a foot deep at the most and that the soil had not even been patted down. Clearing the earth from the body Ed bent and gently lifted out the cadaver and the hat buried alongside it.

The corpse was fully clothed in a patched Reb lieutenant's uniform. Moreover, it was still warm. That suggested to Ed the handsome young man now lying at his feet had not been long dead and that the two bullet holes near the centre of his brisket had been the cause of his violent demise. It was then he remembered the two gunshots he had heard maybe fifteen minutes before the herd started running. Had this fellow inadvertently ridden in on the hanging, tried to intervene and paid the price with his life? It was a possibility Ed knew he had to take seriously.

He searched the youth's pockets. He found a Yanqui dollar, a silver locket with the miniature portrait of a pretty young girl inside, along with a curl of honey-blonde hair. There was a creased, dirty daguerreotype of a well-dressed man and a finely dressed, elegant woman. Written in ink on the back of the daguerreotype were the words: *Mr and*

Mrs Harlan Hascot, Montgomery, State of Alabama, 1861. Taken for their third born, John Mason Hascot, to remind him of the better days to come when the South has won this war and he has returned a hero.

Ed stared down. 'Never happened, did it, boy?' he said quietly.

He continued searching. Soon he found a piece of paper upon which was written *Major Brock Stedman, Lazy S ranch, sited ten miles east of Taylor's Ford, Conner Basin, Texas Panhandle.*

Ed scrubbed the three-day-old grey and black stubble on his stubbornly jutting chin as he read the words. When he had finished, he raised dark brows. 'Well now,' he said, 'that piece of paper could be important.'

He put the boy's property into his range coat pocket. The name Brock Stedman was already making echoes of things not too long past in his mind; things to do with that war. Yeah, Stedman, wasn't he the piece of scum that was reputed to have shown no mercy, killed prisoners out of hand? Didn't that son of a bitch ride with Quantrill? Didn't he take part in the sacking of that Kansas town of Lawrence on 21 August 1863 and the massacre of near all the male population? Ed frowned. But rumour had it that son of a bitch was found among the dead when Quantrill was cornered and killed in Kentucky.

Was the bastard still alive?

Ed pushed the thoughts to the back of his mind for now. There were more important things to attend to; things that would have seemed ridiculous as little as three hours ago, when he had ridden out of base camp to nurse the herd while Tom and the boys ate their fixings and did the chores around camp.

He cut down the bodies and, one by one, hauled them to higher ground for burial because he did not want the river to wash the cadavers away if, or when, the floods came. After that he dragged Lieutenant John Hascot's remains to the site to be buried alongside Tom and the boys. Ed decided it was the least he could do for the youth if his suspicions that he had tried to stop the hangings proved correct. . .

The sun was beginning to set in red, gold and purple when Ed picked up the shovel. He reckoned it would be past midnight before he finished this undertaking, but finish it he would. Then, come first light, he would head for the Clearwater. However, he did not relish delivering the news he would be carrying.

He rammed the shovel deep into the damp soil and prepared to bury his friend Tom Nation, his equally good friend Clay Nash and the boy River Tolland in the cold, damp earth.

CHAPTER EIGHT

Three weeks and four days on.

Back in Clearwater Valley and nearing the T Bar N site, Ed decided the ride north had seemed endless, due to the urgency that burnt like a hot coal within him. Yet, despite the gravity of the news he was carrying, he still took time out to stop at the first large town he came to. A town that had postal facilities so he could mail on the items he had found on John Mason Hascot's body, along with written details of the assumed circumstances of the young Reb lieutenant's death. He used the information he had found on the back of the daguerreotype as the mailing address.

But not knowing the name of the stream by which he had buried the bodies, Ed gave Taylor's Ford as the place to start, then wrote directions on how to reach the burial site, should any existing relatives wish to claim his body, or simply pay their last respects.

Brock Stedman's address, scribbled on the piece of paper he discovered in Hascot's pocket, he made a copy of and then put the original note with the boy's belongings, suggesting, always providing the note reached his relatives, that the Lazy S ranch might be a good place to start. Afterwards, he had tucked Charlie Hibbert's laboriously written bill of sale into one of his two vest pockets because he had the suspicion that one day it might prove to be important.

As he loped the roan up the long Clearwater valley he was heartened to see a newly built and greatly enlarged ranch house was standing big and proud on the old location. Also, that a larger and more comfortable-looking bunkhouse had been constructed. Further to those buildings were other assorted constructions: a smithy, two amply sized barns, three sheds and a triple john. He also noticed all the walls were caulked, ready to defy the worst of Colorado winters. Frank had sure got the job done, Ed decided as he drew ever nearer, though he had never really doubted he would. He knew Tom Nation's dogged determination ran like a bar of steel right through his son's big frame.

When he was close on a hundred yards from the ranch house frontage, Frank came out of the door to stand on the spanking new long gallery that ran the length of the house and the sides facing east and west. Reaching the long rail that fenced the balcony Ed noticed Frank grasped the stout timber bar so tight that his knuckles were white. From that gesture Ed guessed Frank must have been waiting with a deal of impatience for the herd to arrive and was more than likely wondering why Ed Colerich, his second father, came riding in alone.

Standing there tall and strong, young Frank made a fine figure of a man. Blonde-haired, he was six feet two inches in height and had wide, well-muscled shoulders that tapered to slim hips.

And at the moment Frank had a calm look about him. But Ed knew when the younker got real riled up about something these days those grey eyes of his could quickly turn to resemble chips of the purest steel. Potentially killer's eyes, in fact, and all due to that war. Even so, Ed also knew that Frank was trying real hard to get those lethal tendencies under control. Nevertheless, he had grave doubts that Frank would ever get back to being the easy-going fellow he once was. On the other hand, in these untamed Western lands, now made worse by a war that had produced a legion of hard, callous men to whom the dealing of death had little meaning, Ed figured that was no bad thing.

Tired now, for he had been in the saddle since four that morning, Ed eased his roan to a stop and waited for Frank to walk down the three steps that extended out from the gallery. Now on the flat, worn ground before the new T Bar N, Frank strode the eight paces of dusty ground between them. When he reached him he came straight to the point.

'Where are Pa and the boys, Ed – the herd?'

Ed raised grizzled brows. No point in beating around the bush. He told the story, as he knew it. By the time he finished, Frank's stern face had become stone-like and his lips had compressed into a thin, bloodless line. His stare resembled two beads of the purest steel. He must be bearing terrible anguish but Ed knew he would not show it. It was another product of that damned war – a man hiding his true feelings. For, after a while, due to the many ghastly, torn bodies a man saw, death became a familiar sight and ceased to have meaning. It was just a consequence, fetid and horrible. But what it left inside a man was like a festering sore, never truly forgotten.

'All dead you say . . . hung?' Frank said. There was a slight tremor in his voice.

Ed nodded. 'As if they were dogs, and the like of which I never want to see again, unless it's those sons of bitches that did the lynching swinging there.'

Here Ed paused, sighed and rubbed his grizzled chin. He accepted the next piece of information he was about to impart might be even less welcome to Frank, knowing his dislike of Johnny Reb. Even so, he told it. 'Regarding the young Reb lieutenant,' he went on, 'I reburied him along with Tom and the boys. It seemed the right thing to do.'

Frank stared at him for some moments. It was as if he was turning this new, and clearly unexpected, and maybe unwanted, piece of information over in his mind before he gave an answer. The he said, 'So, how d'you figure that was right?'

Ed shrugged. 'Like I explained just now, I got the feeling that maybe the young fella accidentally rode in on the hanging, protested and paid a high price for his objections. Alternatively, I got another notion – he could have already been with the people that took the herd, didn't like what was happening and complained. But no matter what, in my book, those sons of bitches killed him sure enough.'

Frank 'hummed' and rubbed his chin and then sighed. 'Well, I guess we'll never rightly know what happened.'

'Unless we beat it out of the bastards that did it,' Ed said.

Frank stared at him. Fire kindled his blue-grey gaze. He said, 'Yeah, now that would be something.'

Ed now fumbled in his vest pocket, pulled out the copy of Stedman's address and passed it down to Frank. 'I found the original on the youth and copied it before I put it in with his belongings and mailed it. Maybe it's something we can work on.'

Frank took the piece of paper and read it and as he did his already severe face set into ever grimmer lines. He frowned. 'Brock Stedman, didn't he ride with that renegade Quantrill and Bloody Bill Anderson? Evil son of a bitch, by all accounts. I thought he was dead.'

Ed pursed his lips. 'So did I, but you don't hear of many Brock Stedmans – not in my experience anyway.'

Frank said. 'Seems he has given himself a rank.' He narrowed his eyelids. 'You figure it's him that's behind the hangings, old-timer?'

Ed sucked in breath. 'Can't be sure, but he's hot favourite in my book, judging from what we know so far. And those beeves we bought did have the Lazy S brand on them, but that doesn't necessarily make Stedman guilty of taking them. However, like I say, I have my suspicions.'

Frank thoughtfully rubbed his chin before he said, 'It sure is something to think hard on.'

Ed nodded. 'Yeah, and that's what I've been doing on the ride up and I'm now telling you my conclusions.'

Ed eased in the saddle to relieve his aching limbs. Hell, he was not a young man any more and it had been a long, hard ride to Texas and back. He also felt he could sleep for a week after the urgency he had put into this return ride. Even so, he pulled out the bill of sale he had found in the dirt by the stream, bent down and gave it to Frank. 'This here is the note given to your pa as proof of sale by Charlie Hibbert in the Blue Star saloon at Taylor's Ford. As you can see, it also clearly says those beeves were once part of Lazy S stock.'

Ed stopped briefly and spat into the dust. 'Maybe Stedman is pulling some kind of racket. Or maybe Hibbert stole those beeves and Stedman thought Tom and the boys had taken them and then hung them for Yanqui rustlers because of it. Whichever way it was, for some reason young John Hascot must have come out against the hangings and, as I say, paid the price for his dissent.' Ed now looked Frank squarely in the eye. 'I tell you, Frank, even as a corpse he looked a personable young man and not likely to take to sharp practice.'

After seeming to digest the news, Frank took a deep breath. 'Well, whatever way it was, for me this whole thing is beginning to have a strong smell of dirty work about it.' He looked up, his stare made serious with intent. 'We're going back, old-timer,' he said, 'you know that. We owe it to Pa and the boys.'

Once more Ed spat on to the dry ground and eyed Frank keenly. 'I sure would have been mighty disappointed if you'd said otherwise, son, and that's a fact.'

Fondness now replaced the hard stare that was natural to Frank these days and a faint smile spread across his lips as he raised his blonde brows. 'So what the hell you still sitting that horse for, old-timer? Climb down, Goddamnit.'

Ed pursed his lips before he grinned wryly. 'Past three months or so I've kind of got glued to this saddle. Seems real unnatural not to be in it.'

He began to climb down, grunting as the arthritics began to stab pain into his knees as well as most other parts of his body. He grimaced. If truth be known, though he was not what you would call old yet, a hard life had worn him down and the often terrible conditions he had endured during that war hadn't helped either.

Three hands – he knew them – were coming from different parts of the ranch environs now: from the new bunkhouse, from one of the large new barns, from the corrals near the river that ran by the ranch. The cottonwoods, aspen, birch and willow that lined that stream, he noticed, were now rich with the reds, golds and yellows of the fall. The sight heartened him and filled him with nostalgia for the old days before that damned war.

Brad Sadler was the first to reach them. Brad was tall and thin as a beanpole. He had a mop of ginger hair and was blind in the left eye, due to being hit by shrapnel in the bloody battle for Vicksburg. But the nasty wound did not hinder his shooting abilities. The sliver of steel had also left a vivid scar down the side of his face, giving his features a vicious, ugly look, which did not match his character. Brad could be the mildest of men until roused. Then he could be hell on high wheels. Brad said, 'I heard part of what you were saying, Ed. God Almighty, Tom and the boys dead?'

'That's the size of it.'

Ed continued to work his knees and other joints and grimaced all the time as the pain sawed through them. Dammit, he should be thinking of retiring from the saddle; he should be thinking of opening a saloon somewhere and making things a little easier for himself.

However, he knew he would never do that. He was part of the T Bar N; he always had been and always would be. His heart, bones – his very soul – was in every rock, blade of grass and tall timber of this land. And after the tragic death of Tom's wife, Mary, he had given his life to it and to his great friend Tom Nation. So how could a man stop his *life*, for God's sake? On top of that, there was unfinished business down there on the Texas Panhandle.

The other two men walking in from the outbuildings Ed knew to be Jim Daltry and Carl Hollis. Both were war veterans; both were Clearwater Basin men who had ridden for the T Bar N before that war and both had signed up to fight the cause. Clearly, Frank, having discovered they were back in the valley, had recruited them to help rebuild the ranch. On arriving, Jim Daltry gave Ed his full attention – the look on his moon face and in his brown eyes clearly puzzled as he said, 'Where's Tom, Ed. . . ? The boys?'

'Dead,' Frank intervened.

His blunt answer caused Daltry and Hollis to turn their stares towards him. Then Daltry bowed his head. 'Oh! Jesus!'

Ed could see both men were completely taken aback. Frank repeated the story. When he'd finished, Carl Hollis shook his head. 'And here's me thinking Ed was riding ahead with good news.'

Frank looked meaningfully at the three men. 'Ed and me are going back, boys; d'you want to ride along?'

The men stared at each other as if each were seeking to know the other's thinking. Then, as if they had come to a corporate agreement, Carl Hollis said, 'Guess it wouldn't be right if we didn't, boss. Tom was a fine man and a fine boss. Sure didn't deserve to die like that.'

Brad Sadler cleared his throat then as though he wanted to add something to that. 'But we'll face big odds from what I've heard so far,' he said.

Frank gazed at him with understanding before he said, 'Feel free to stand aside, Brad. Nobody'll think the worse of you. We all know your war record.'

Sadler's single-eyed look was one of deep resentment as he said, 'Jesus, Frank, that's not what I meant at all. I was just being realistic. Dammit, you got to be that. Hell, I rode for your pa for ten years before the war. He was the finest boss a man could ever wish for. Just try leaving me out, is all.'

Frank nodded his satisfaction; he even smiled a little. 'Truth be known, never truly figured otherwise, Brad.'

He turned now and Ed met his steady gaze. 'Reckon I'll ride up to Ma's grave now, old-timer – just for an hour or two.'

Ed nodded gravely. 'She'll want to know, if she don't already. Like the Injuns, I got a firm belief that such things are possible.' He squinted now against the bright sun as he stared at Frank. 'You want me to ride along, son?'

Frank shook his head. 'No. Get yourself some feed, and some rest. And ask one of the boys to look after your horse; he looks real worn down.'

Ed admitted, 'I did push him hard.'

Frank now looked at Sadler, Daltry and Hollis in turn. 'We'll be bringing them all home, boys,' he said, 'Tom, Clay and River. They'll be buried in T Bar N soil or I'll die in the trying.'

Sadler looked at him queerly before he said, 'Can't be no other way.' Jim Daltry said, 'Hell it don't need to be said. Tom Nation belongs in Clearwater soil, no doubt about it; so do those boys.'

Frank nodded, satisfaction clearly on his determined face.

Ed now looked keenly at him. 'You all right, boy?' he said. 'I mean, about your pa?'

Instantly, affection registered on Frank's formidable features. 'No, I ain't,' he said, 'but I'll deal with it, old friend, just like you've had to do.'

Ed said, 'D'you want me to ride into town, then, after I've eaten? Figure somebody ought to tell Jenny Tolland about her boy.'

Frank pursed his lips for a moment before he said, 'My job, old-timer; got to be now Pa's not with us.'

Ed's stare was candid. 'You know you've got some mighty big boots to fill, boy.'

Frank nodded. 'I know, but I'll fill them.'

Ed smiled. 'Yeah, reckon you will at that,' he said.

As for informing Clay Nash's kin . . . Ed pursed his lips. As far as he knew Clay did not have any relations, never mentioned any, anyway. He just showed up at the T Bar N eighteen years ago, asked for a job and stayed. Ed always got the impression Clay considered the riders at the T Bar N was all the family he'd ever need. As for River Tolland's demise . . . a boy of sixteen? Well, there sure needed to be a reckoning on that one when they got to Texas.

It was then that Ed heard a woman singing, a sweet, full, melodious voice, a voice, he realized, he had not heard in four years. Moments later, Amy Killeen appeared at the ranch house door. She was wiping her hands on a large white cloth. She was older now by four years, but, Ed decided, that didn't make a deal of difference; she was still the girl with the gold-red hair, the green eyes, the trim waist and full lips; the one who had been madly in love with Frank. Also, she was the one that had been called upon to sing at every concert and hoedown there ever was in Brightwater Basin. 'Well now,' he said. He turned his gaze to Frank, making it very clear he was delighted to hear the trilling but that he also wanted answers.

Melting his grim look Frank said, 'Came riding down two days after you, Pa and the boys left for Texas, carrying a can of antelope stew and a suitcase with her clothes in it. She dumped her case on the grass, then announced that was where it stayed until she got the right answer out of me and after she'd got that she was never going to lose sight of me ever again, choose what. It was after that little drama I figured the only thing I could respectfully do was to call in the preacher from Three Pines and marry her and then get the ranch built as quickly as possible.'

Ed still grinned his pleasure. 'Well, dammit, that's the first sensible thing you've ever done in my book!'

'She never gave up on me,' Frank went on as though he was still surprised by the iron tenacity shown by some women when the time came to reveal their undying love for their chosen man.

'Well, I never doubted it for one second, son,' Ed said still showing his glee with a grin. 'And, by God, I reckon Tom would've been over the moon had he lived to see this day.'

Instantly, Frank's grin faded. 'Yeah,' he said, with a

long, heavy sigh 'reckon he would at that, old-timer.'

Ed wanted to say sorry for bringing back memories, but he didn't. A silence lay between them,. then Frank looked up and said, 'Come and say hello, old-timer,' before he turned and looked at Jim Daltry. 'Look after Ed's horse, uh, Jim?'

'Sure thing.' Daltry took the worn reins on the roan and walked away to the new barn.

Despite the sadness of his homecoming the delight Ed now felt was unabated. He had known Amy Killeen most of her life. The Killeens had settled the northern end of the basin four years after Tom put down roots at the southern end. From day one it had been an amicable relationship that had endured.

When they reached Amy she said, clearly with anxiety, 'Frank, where's Tom . . . the boys?'

Frank told the story. When he was finished she ran into his arms and clasped him tightly. 'Oh! Dear God!' Frank held her while she sobbed into his chest. After minutes of clear grief she leaned back and stared at him with wet, tragic eyes. 'And my own pa isn't back yet. Oh! Frank, that terrible war! Damn Crook! Damn Robert E. Lee! Damn all politicians! They've taken near all we hold dear.'

Frank patted her gently on the back. 'There now, honey,' he said, 'your pa's a tough customer. He'll be back, you see.'

'But what about Jack and Fred, my other brothers?' Amy sobbed. Her gaze was tragic as it looked up into her husband's eyes.

Frank continued to pat her. 'They're survivors, honey. Just believe in them.'

But Amy's look remained appalled. 'Easy to say!' Then her features altered. 'Oh! Frank, I'm sorry! Here's me going on when you've lost *all* you have!'

'Not quite, honey,' Frank said quietly, 'I've got you and I've got Ed here. This old-timer's allus been like a second father to me. And on top of that, we got a ranch to build up. Pa would have wanted us to make it like it once was.'

'But,' Amy said, 'you've lost all your stock.'

'Yeah, well, I'm figuring on doing something about that real sharp,' Frank said.

Amy went quiet, as if at a loss to give sane meaning to it all, and again buried her face into Frank's chest. Ed looked significantly at Frank, hopefully indicating he'd like to know what had happened to the Killeen family. Frank continued to stroke his wife's gold-red locks and held her close. But he whispered, 'Talk to you later, old-timer.'

Ed nodded and went over to the cook shack, see if there was any leftover food. There was: beef stew. While he warmed it up on the still hot stove he watched Frank lead Amy into the house. Minutes later, he came out of the fine dwelling and saddled up a lively piebald and urged it up the knoll toward the family gravesite. After a short while he saw Amy come out and walk toward the cook shack. Reaching the door she poked her head in and said, 'Eat at the house, Ed.'

'The beef stew's fine, Amy,' he said.

Frank's new wife persisted. 'Even so, bring it along to the house; I want to tell you about Pa and my brothers.'

Had her intuition – most women seemed to be endowed with that strange facility – told her of his unspoken desire to know about her family's misfortunes? Ed raised grizzled brows; he was unsure about stirring up more unhappy memories for the girl right now, which would surely surface if she were to tell the story.

But he said, 'Sure, if it'll help.'

'It will,' Amy said firmly.

Seated on the cowhide settee in the big new common room that smelled sweetly of freshly cut pine, Ed waited while Amy settled herself in the rocker by the window. Now silhouetted in the bright light coming through the glazed port and rocking gently in the rocker, she looked at him with candid green eyes and began to tell her story. Last she heard, her father was at Camp Cousins, Massachusetts, recovering from a bad shoulder wound. Jack and Fred, the eldest brothers, she had not heard from for over a year. Jeremiah, the youngest, and Ernie the next youngest, were back at the Circle K. Ernie had returned with only one arm, the right one. But, she added proudly, he was not letting it get in the way of doing chores around the place. Every day he was learning more ways to cope with his disability.

Then she went quiet. Despite putting a brave face on things, the situation regarding her family was clearly hurting her badly. On impulse, Ed reached over and grasped her right hand and patted it.

'Things'll work out, Amy,' he said, 'you see. Your men are a tough bunch.'

Amy looked at him, her green gaze direct. 'Frank keeps telling me that.' But she said it as if she did not believe it. She took a deep breath and added, 'What d'you think Frank will do about his pa?'

Ed shrugged. 'Figure it best if he told you that, girl.'

'He's going to Texas, isn't he?'

Ed stared at her pretty, yet determined face. 'Knowing Frank, I reckon you know the answer to that as well as I do.'

Her look was not a happy one, but she said, 'Yeah, guess I do.' She smiled wistfully. 'Well, thanks for taking the time to talk, Ed.'

Ed shrugged once more. 'Isn't a lot to be said, right now. That war wrecked most of our lives and is still doing it, seems to me.'

After a few minutes he let go of her hand and headed for the new bunkhouse and some much-needed sleep.

He was awake when Frank got back to the T Bar N. It was close on six in the evening. Over supper Frank related where he had been and what he had been doing. He had visited his mother's grave and then he had gone on into Three Pines to break the news to Jenny Tolland about her boy's death. He had given her what pay was due to River and a hundred dollars besides to help tide her over. However, he could do nothing about the grief she obviously felt.

After supper, Frank decided to call a meeting regarding the trip to Texas. He invited Jim Daltry, Brad Sadler and Cal Hollis to sit in and give their opinions on how they should go about the venture.

It proved to be a lively gathering. Largely, with Frank's strong guidance, they came to the opinion that when they got to Texas they should keep a low profile until they'd gathered enough information to act. All wanted retribution; all wanted the herd back and all knew what odds they were likely to face when the need for action came.

It was 3.30 a.m when Ed collapsed into a dreamless sleep that lasted for ten hours.

CHAPTER NINE

Five and one other – Amy Nation, née Killeen – were now across the Colorado-Texas line and heading for Taylor's Ford, via the no-name stream. Collars up, they were riding into a raw wind that chapped their faces and numbed their hands. Soon they came to the back of the butte from the top of which Ed had watched the herd being taken, then they eased their way around its piney base.

Here, Ed pulled rein and stared down the mile and a half long grassy slope to the now leafless, tree-lined creek where he, Tom, and the boys had made their last camp. He could see the stream, now dull grey under these leaden skies. He turned to Frank and pointed. 'That's where I buried them.'

Frank nodded. His look bleak, he stared long and hard at the place indicated. Amy was sitting her pinto by his side. Tenderly she took hold of his arm, her look one of deep concern, but Frank smiled and gently patted her hand.

'It's OK, honey. I'm fine.'

Though the caress was a loving one, Ed knew Frank

would have greatly preferred to have left Amy behind. In fact, he had insisted in no uncertain terms that she obey him. However, he was finding she had the kind of resolution that near matched his own. And, to Ed's mind, back at the T Bar N she had clearly brooded on his strictures the whole fortnight they used to make the arrangements and preparations needed before leaving for Texas.

It was on departure day, sitting her pinto while she watched them fill the water butts at the river, that she finally sprung her intentions upon Frank.

'Husband,' she said, 'no matter what you have demanded of me to do while you're gone, I've decided I'm not going to let you out of my sights ever again, choose what you're riding into. I'm going to Texas with you and that is that!'

Frank stiffened and stared at her, amazed. But to demonstrate she meant every word of what she said she got down off her pinto and tied it to the rear of the wagon. Then she climbed up onto the wagon loaded with food supplies and other things useful on the trail and settled her shapely denim-clad backside onto the wooden driving seat. Then she grabbed the reins off the brake stick and stared at her obviously astonished husband and said, 'So, fill those water butts, Goddamnit, and let's get the show on the road!'

When Frank was sufficiently recovered it was like a dam had been broken. He said, 'Woman, have you gone crazy? Guns are going to be popping off down there; men are likely to get killed. And who's going to look after the ranch while we're gone, for Chris'sake?'

She stared her contempt at his apparent lack of knowledge of her abilities. 'Husband, regarding guns . . . I've been hearing them go off most of my life, done some shooting myself, as you well know. As for the ranch . . . well, I've thought about that, too, and I've asked my brothers to look in on the place now and again while we're gone. I've also asked those two old-timers in Three Pines, George Shaw and Percy Nelson, to live on the place and generally feed the livestock we bought to sustain us – the pigs, chickens, milk cows and so forth – and do whatever other chores need to be done until we return. I reckon that should be enough, don't you?'

'Enough?' Frank roared. There was a brief, fuming silence before he continued, 'By God, woman, it seems to me we've got a lot to talk about as to who is going to wear the britches around here!'

Amy again tilted her chin. 'There'll be no need. Husband, when this trouble is over that will be you. But until then I'm having it *my* way, y'hear?'

Still clearly seething with pent-up frustration Frank looked ferociously at his defiant wife, but he seemed at a loss as to what to say. Finally he declared, 'Oh, to hell with it! We've wasted enough time. But, by God, lady, this ain't over!'

As if with finality, Amy said, 'It is as far as I'm concerned.'

However, Frank hardly heard her reply. He dug boot heels unnecessarily hard into the flanks of his big roan gelding he called Hercules. The beast grunted and turned to stare at him with what could be only construed as injured surprise before getting into its stride.

Ed was also taken aback by such harsh treatment. Frank

had had that handsome roan a number of years, from a colt, to be precise. They were real buddies. More, the horse had got him out of more than one tight fix during that war just gone. And right now the beast was clearly resenting Frank's odd behaviour. Hercules had been a real pal to that boy and he should never forget that.

Thinking back now on that clash of wills and sitting his horse and staring at the creek a mile yonder down the slope, Ed found humour was still to be had out of that brisk exchange. Further, Amy wasn't driving the wagon any more; Brad Sadler was. And it had been that way for most of the ride down. It seemed that girl just liked to sit a saddle and scout and be like one of the boys.

They moved steadily down the long slope. Reaching the gurgling stream they pulled rein and stared at the still undisturbed rocks that spelled out the warning: DEATH TO ALL YANQUI RUSTLERS. Then they rode up the slope to where the graves were and dismounted. Brad Sadler climbed down off the wagon, wrapped the reins around the brake handle and walked up behind them.

Now ranked across the east side of the graves, each man took off his hat and offered his own particular prayer to the dead. After a couple of minutes Frank lifted his head, replaced his worn, sweat-greased hat, and stared at the now grass-grown mounds of earth. 'We've come to get 'em, Pa,' he said quietly. Ed met his bleak stare as he turned to him. 'Now, take us to Taylor's Ford, old-timer.'

Ed nodded, his satisfaction warm within him. 'It'll be my pleasure.' He turned his stocky chestnut back down the slope and splashed across the stream. The others followed.

Entering Taylor's Ford, Ed found the town hadn't changed much from the time he, Tom and the boys had ridden in to buy cattle from Charley Hibbert. The Blue Star saloon, where the deal to buy the herd had been hammered out, was more or less in the centre of town. Chiefly the settlement's make-up was a wide, wheel-rutted street bordered by a spread-out bunch of clapboard dwellings and business premises, half of which were boarded up. When Ed, those months ago, asked why so many houses in town were empty, he received a reply of, 'Because they belong to folks that ain't got back from the war yet and maybe never will.' Ed pursed his lips and gazed around. It seemed things had not changed much here at Taylor's Ford.

The group tied up at the Blue Star seven-horse tie rail, dusted down and walked in through the swing doors. Being just after mid-morning the place was almost empty. Ed counted seven customers: four card-playing *hombres* and two men drinking and talking cagily in the gloomy far right corner of the establishment; there was also a tall, lean handsome-looking fellow sitting alone drinking coffee and smoking a cheroot in the left far corner. He made a striking figure of a man, a fellow not easily forgotten. And, as Ed expected, all the occupants looked long and hard at them before settling back to what they had been doing. Well, all but the tall, lean fellow drinking his coffee. His scrutiny stayed longest of all.

Frank ordered whiskey all round and then asked Amy what she preferred. She stared at him as if hugely surprised. Revealing her red-gold hair in all its glory she pushed her worn, wide-brimmed hat back onto her shoulders.

'Why, the same as you, Goddamnit,' she said.

'You only used to drink sarsaparilla,' Frank said, frowning.

'Time and wars can change a girl,' Amy said.

The reply amazed nobody for, on the ride down, Amy proved to be a real mixture and, Frank found, not at all like the girl he'd left behind. Oh, she was still soft and gentle in many ways, as a woman should be, Ed conceded, and generally domesticated, but she did have this hard core. In fact she rode like a cowboy, fired her Colt .36 Army like a cowboy, spat like a cowboy, talked like a cowboy and took her knocks like a cowboy. As she explained, to get it out of the way once and for all, she could be no other way. She had been brought up alongside four rough-and-tumble brothers, had been born near sitting a saddle and had ridden four years as a full-blown Circle K ranch-hand because of that war. She even claimed she could probably drink half of them under the table if it ever came down to that.

Frank offered her a wide grin and answered her. 'You can, huh?' He turned to the barkeep. 'So, whiskey it is for the little lady, too.'

'And not so much of the Goddamned little, either,' Amy said.

Ed had to chuckle inwardly. Feisty was the word for Amy Nation these days, he decided, and, if he remembered aright, always had been. And, as she so robustly claimed, she wasn't so small. Ed knew her height to be five feet ten inches, which was mighty tall for a woman. Five foot nothing to four was usually the norm. On top of that she was strong, though her strength did not spoil her feminine lines, nor her graceful way of moving. But hopefully, when the responsibility of children and running a busy ranch house came along it would bring out the latent domesticity in the girl and subdue her tendency toward masculinity. He'd seen such a thing happen on more than one occasion in a long and varied life. However, right now, truth be said, Amy Nation was a joyful handful.

The burly bartender placed six shots glasses along the bar and left the bottle, then went back to reading a dog-eared Eastern magazine, maybe six months old. Second bottle round Amy got to singing. Her dulcet tones brought to a stop the card game and the *hombres* quietly talking at the table in the right corner. The man sipping coffee in the left corner took his attention off his coffee cup and stared. All were now listening with rapt attention and maybe dreaming of better days gone by. Ed knew even the hardest of cases were known to melt when some songbird trilled a particularly homely song. Amy's melodic warbling even brought the rotund Jack O'Brian, the owner of the Blue Star, out of his small office at the rear of the premises, to lean on the far end of the bar and listen intently while speculatively chewing on the long, thin stogie stuck between his generous purple lips.

Amy finished her song with a smile and a flourish. All stood, cards neglected, talk and coffee forgotten, to wave their hats, or clap their hands, or whoop their applause. Ed also saw the folks that had been walking past outside had stopped to crowd around the swing doors to listen. They, too, were clapping approvingly as the last notes of Amy's song died away. Clearly, Taylor's Ford had been starved of quality entertainment for some time.

As the acclaim died down Jack O'Brian took the stogie out of his mouth. His red, round face beaming, his blue eyes shining with appreciation, he stepped forward and took Amy's right hand enthusiastically in both of his. 'My dear lady,' he said, 'allow me to introduce myself. My name is Jack O'Brian. I own this place. Now, permit me to say you sing like a nightingale and that that observation inevitably prompts the question . . would you be looking for a job now?'

'Maybe not,' Frank said, stepping forward aggressively.

Amy glared at her husband before turning back to O'Brian to say, 'That will depend on the terms, sir.'

O'Brian beamed a smile and revealed even, but tobacco-yellowed teeth. 'Of course! Would we have it any other way, my dear.'

Clearly angry now, Frank hissed in Amy's ear, 'We need to talk about this, girl; right now.'

Amy's stare was defiant before she turned and smiled sweetly at the Irishman saying, 'Will you excuse us for a moment, Mr O'Brian?'

The saloon owner spread his arms. 'Why, of course, ma'am.'

Frank was already leading her away by the arm. When they were out of earshot he said, 'Just what in tarnation you playing at, lady?'

It was always 'lady' when her husband was angry.

Amy gave him a look of exasperation. 'Think about it, Frank; where is all the range gossip in a small town exchanged, uh? In the general store or the main saloon, right? And what do we want right now? *Information.*'

Frank paddled on battered size ten boots and tugged

irritably at his worn hat brim. 'Even so, I don't like it. It ain't fitting for a wife of mine to be—'

Amy said, 'What's the matter, don't you trust me?'

'Sure I trust you,' Frank said. 'Nevertheless, as I was about to say, I just don't want my *new wife*, remember, working in some damned saloon to be pawed over by any Tom, Dick or Harry that comes into the place.'

'I can take care of myself,' Amy said. 'It won't happen.'

'I still don't like it, Goddamnit!' Frank shouted. Clearly his temper had snapped and had caused him to forget his need for discretion.

And as if he had been eavesdropping Jack O'Brian said, 'The little lady will be well looked after, sir; I will personally guarantee it.'

Frank stared, his look fierce. 'You been listening to us?'

O'Brian spread his hands. 'Lord no, sir,' he said. 'Only you raised your voice and I could not help but overhear.'

Frank seemed to calm down. 'Yeah, well, we ain't sure we're staying yet, mister. You got that?'

Clear disappointment filled the Irishman's face. He said, 'Ah! Now that would be a pity, sir. A nightingale like the little lady would make her the toast of the territory in no time at all. A sweeter voice I've never heard, and I've heard quite a few in my time, I can tell you.'

He paused and screwed up fatty eyelids. 'If it is not too impertinent a question, sir, would the little lady be your wife by any chance?'

'You ask too many questions, friend,' Frank said, 'and that ain't a healthy thing to do these parts, as you should well know.'

O'Brian said. 'Indeed I do and once nearly to my cost.

But by that, can I take it that she is?'

Amy intervened, smiling sweetly before glaring at Frank. 'You can, sir, and we will think about your offer. However, if you don't mind, I'm not your little lady.'

O'Brian raised thick black brows. 'Ah! I see the description grates upon your ear. Then 'tis my mistake, ma'am, and will not be repeated.' He paused to eye her up and down before he added, 'Indeed, *statuesque* would be a more fitting word for you, I think.'

Frank paced forward, fists clenched. 'You being rude, mister?' Amy whispered, with some exasperation, 'It's a compliment, Frank.' She turned and again smiled engagingly at the saloon owner. 'We'll contact you in due course, Mr O'Brian. And thank you for your kind words.'

O'Brian waved his cigar dismissively. 'Nothing but the truth, ma'am,' he said. 'Now, when can I expect a reply? I need to spread the news, though, I guess, what has been heard so far will already be setting the prairie on fire.'

Before Amy could reply, Frank said, 'Like the lady said, we'll think about it. Now, we need accommodation. You got any suggestions, O'Brian?'

The Irishman wafted an arm toward the grey overcast outside. 'Why, there's a whole passel of empty dwellings out there, friend,' he said. 'You can take your pick. But a word of warning; you will need to vacate if the owners come back.'

Frank nodded. 'Understood.' He turned and looked down the line of his riders. 'OK, boys, let's find a place to live.'

It was just then that words came from one of the two men sitting in the far corner. 'Hold on. Ain't sure you'd be made welcome here, Yanqui.'

Frank turned to face a slack-mouthed, spotty-chinned, grinning youth standing by the table he'd been sitting at talking to the *hombre* who was now lounging back in his chair. Frank observed the two ivory-handled .36 Colt Navy cap-and-balls around the youth's waist – one holstered and one stuck in his belt. He also eyed up the sheathed Bowie knife that was stuck in the top of his right boot. It was clear by the way the brat carried those weapons that he was no stranger to their use. At the same time, Ed was observing the other man who had been seated with the grinning brat and was now cleaning his fingernails with a clasp knife and occasionally staring up at them. There was something familiar about the man, he thought. Dammit, what was it?

Meanwhile, Frank was saying, 'Ain't looking for your opinion, boy.'

'Pay you to heed it, all the same,' Kat Malling said.

'The war's over, friend,' Frank said.

Malling grinned. 'So I heard. Pity some folks don't know it.'

'Like you?' Frank said.

Malling smiled. 'Like me.'

'Too bad,' Frank said. He turned to his men. 'Come on, boys.'

'Hold it.' Malling's voice now had an icy ring to it. 'It's good advice I'm giving you, friend. Ride on.'

'I don't take advice from strangers,' Frank said. 'Good or bad.'

'Now that's a pity.'

Frank stared. 'Save your pity for others, we don't need it.' He turned and walked unhurriedly towards the open doors. 'Come on, boys.'

Daltry, Hollis, Amy and Sadler followed, but Ed hung out at the their backs, eyeing the pimply, grinning bastard who was watching their departure. However, the skinny youth made no bad moves and Ed followed the boys out.

At the tie rail Frank said, 'OK, boys, mount up and fan out and look for suitable properties. We'll meet up in half an hour, outside the hardware store.' He waved a hand at the low wooden building fifty yards up the street, announcing the legend: Lightfoot's Supplies, Service and Quality Guaranteed. It was then the fellow who had been cleaning his fingernails while the pimply bastard talked came out of the swing doors and presented himself.

'Gents, name's Charley Hibbert.'

Ed felt a tingle run down his spine. Sure he was. Why had he not recognized Hibbert in the saloon just now? Because the fellow had shaved off his beard, therefore making himself look completely different. And on hearing the name Ed noticed Frank stiffen, too. But he said, affably enough, 'Howdy? Anything we can do for you?'

Hibbert smiled disarmingly. 'I shouldn't take too much notice of Kat Malling in there. Gets a little scratchy when he's had too much to drink.'

'That could get him killed,' Frank said. He added, 'Now, is that all, friend?'

Hibbert said, 'No, indeedy. No, sir.' He turned and looked around at Ed and the boys who, after hearing his name, were now eyeing him up carefully.

He raised his battered hat and grinned. 'And howdy, y'all!' he said. Then he returned his gaze to Frank. 'Now, you look like cattlemen to me, sir, and if you're buying I've got beeves in the hills just waiting for a customer. They're all prime stock and I want to get them off my hands before winter comes. Maybe we could do a deal?'

Frank's gaze studied the man's smiling face. Hibbert had a low forehead, long, oily-looking brown hair, tanned, drawn skin and dark stubble on his chin. His black eyes moved constantly in their sunken sockets and when he smiled he showed black and broken teeth.

Frank said, 'Maybe. I'll bear you in mind.'

Hibbert said, 'Already got one or two offers. . . .'

Frank said, 'Then don't wait for me.'

Hibbert held up his hand. 'Don't be too hasty. Maybe you'll change your mind when you see them.' Then he frowned and swivelled his eyes to Ed. 'Don't I know you from someplace, friend?'

'Guess not,' Ed said. 'Ain't been in this country before.'

Hibbert nodded. 'Maybe I'm mistaken.' He turned and undid the piebald tied to the seven-horse rail and mounted. Seated in the saddle he said, 'If you change your mind I'm easy to find. Ask anybody. Charlie Hibbert.'

'I'll remember that,' Frank said.

'Be to your advantage, friend,' Hibbert said then he replaced his shabby hat and touched the brim. '*Adios*, for now.'

He rode away, northwest.

His eyes following him, Frank smiled grimly as he turned to Ed. 'By God, this gets better,' he said. 'I figure Mr Hibbert will be able to help us more than somewhat. Guess it would pay to visit sometime. Meanwhile, let's find a place to shelter and make ourselves at home.'

CHAPTER TEN

They found a big house on the outskirts; five rooms in all. It needed a little fixing but it would do. Amy bought supplies from Jeremy Lightfoot, owner of the store situated in the centre of town, and with help loaded them onto the wagon. Nobody questioned what they were doing. They already seemed to know. And Lightfoot was only too willing to make the sale, Yanqui dollars now being the legal currency. Meantime, one of the boys stoked up the oven they found intact in what had to be the kitchen of the house.

By dusk there was the aroma of frying bacon and eggs sizzling in the skillet. A huge saucepan of spiced up beans was also bubbling on top of the oblong stove. A long wooden table in the middle of the large kitchen and long bench seats, which were drawn up along either side, were covered with years of dust before the boys cleaned it off. They appeared to have stood there for years, undisturbed. Brad Sadler found a lamp in one of the rooms. He trimmed the wick and filled it with coal oil purchased from Jeremy Lightfoot. It lit the kitchen real well and it was happy bunch that sat down to dine that night.

As for the horses, there was a large abandoned barn a hundred yards from the back of the house. They bedded them down in there for the night and fed them hay bought from Jesse Hart who ran the livery stables a half mile north of town. They got water from the thirty-foot deep communal well, in the centre of town. Taylor's Ford must have been a reasonably prosperous place before that war sent everybody's lives all to hell, Ed decided.

They were clearing away the enamel crocks and placing them in the large galvanized sink fastened to the south wall when, without warning, a barrage of shots came raging in out of the darkness. Glass shattered and razor-sharp slivers flew across the room.

Reacting like a man half his age Ed blew out the oil lamp and then, drawing his Colt Army, dived to the dust-layered board floor. Only the oblong oven gave out any sort of light now. Lead was pinging off the iron, showering sparks. Somebody behind him cried out in pain.

Ed turned and crawled across the floor. He found Carl Hollis lying by the door leading out into the narrow, dark hall. Even in the now dust-laden gloom, Ed could see that Carl had a hole in his chest and that he was losing too much blood. He said, 'How bad is it, Carl?'

Hollis grimaced. 'Reckon I'll live. Goddamnit, get to shooting, Ed. Get those lousy bastards!'

Ed doubted Hollis's optimism, having seen an abundance of death-dealing wounds during that war, but you never knew. He also knew Hollis was a real tough *hombre.*

Ed was heading for one of the shattered windows when Jim Daltry grabbed him by the arm. 'I'll cover the front.'

Ed nodded. 'You're thinking right, Jim.'

Daltry disappeared into the darkness of the hall, Henry rifle gripped in his right hand. Ed ducked as more lead ripped through the broken windows and buzzed like angry bees across the room into the already scarred back wall. He made for the nearest window. Amy was already there, calmly firing her Colt. Ed got his own weapon blazing. He aimed at the flashes of gunfire that were spurting like lances of fire out of the dark shrouding the big barn. He could hear the horses were making one hell of a noise in there because of the racket outside. A quick glance around told him Brad Sadler was kneeling by the bullet-smashed window to his left. Frank, he observed, was lying flat by the half-open door. He was using the doorjamb as protection and was firing through the gap made in the doorway.

Ed wanted to know the situation out there, so risking being shot in the head he peered over the shattered window's edge longer than he ought to. Against the previously overcast but now clearer sky, he saw a bright half-moon was floating across the starlit heavens, casting silver light over the scene. Only occasionally did the scurrying clouds hide the lunar glow.

Amid the swirling gunsmoke, Ed saw several men crouched low behind all available cover. The flashes from their guns were vivid against the night sky. Ed got off two shots. It was then two riders came, riding hard, out from behind the barn. They were carrying blazing torches.

God almighty!

It didn't need a man to make two guesses at what was going to happen next. Though the riders were shrouded in the ever-thickening powder smoke, Ed sighted on one of the racing figures and unleashed a shot. He missed. He cocked ready to fire again when the chance presented itself but the riders now separated and swung wide then swerved in, each racing in from opposite directions.

Gunfire was now raging from the house windows. Why weren't they dropping? Those riders must be living a charmed life.

When they got close they swung the torches, lobbing them towards the tinder-dry clapboards. Once more, Ed got one in his sights, but when he pulled the trigger it clicked metallically.

Empty!

One of the firebrands thudded against the outer wall to lie blazing while the other one roared in through the right-hand bullet-shattered window. It flew over his and Amy's heads before skidding off the table to finish blazing between Carl Hollis's legs, near the crotch. At once, flames started eating at the wounded man. Rearing up from his prone position, Carl gave out a harsh cry as he tried to beat out the flames.

Without thinking, Ed jumped up, ran across the room. He grasped the non-burning end of the brand, called out for Amy to duck and flung it out of window. He stared in disbelief as chance caused the flying torch to hit one of the riders full in the face. He screamed as flames enveloped his bearded features.

The fellow began pawing madly at the flames but by that time the brand was falling onto his horse's neck. It stayed there precariously balanced for several moments. Startled by the sudden arrival of the fire, the horse squealed, took the bit and ran into the night, the rider vainly trying to control it.

Ed returned to the window, crouched and loaded his Colt with one of three preloaded cylinders he carried in pouches purposely sewn into his belt for that purpose. It was a trick he had learned after seeing the arrangement on one dead Johnny Reb during that war.

Armed again, he placed the used cylinder on the empty pouch and listened. From the front of the house he could hear Jim Daltry blazing away with his Henry rifle. A steady, reliable man was Jim. He would hold his corner. But back here, the roar of guns was intensifying. Again, risking a look, Ed saw three of the raiders were now trying to get into the barn while the rest provided covering fire.

The horses, Ed thought, *they were after the damned horses!*

The rate of fire from the house heightened immediately. Ed knew that an iron bar slotted across the middle held the barn doors closed. Nevertheless, the raiders were having little trouble disposing of it. They entered the building. It wasn't long before the T Bar N remuda came thundering out through the doors and off into the night. But the manoeuvre had cost the raiders. Two of them were wounded, writhing on the ground in pain. Even so, the T Bar N horses were running God knew where and that had to be bad.

The rest of the raiders were now sprinting for the back of the barn, firing lead over their shoulders. Two stopped to help the wounded men gain shelter. After a minute or so they reappeared, beating their mounts after the T Bar N remuda. The two injured men were swaying drunkenly in their saddles. Nevertheless, they were managing to stay aloft. Then all went quiet. There was only the occasional exasperated shot chasing after them into the darkness. Gone! The night was now near silent and the air was filled only with wreathing gunsmoke after the discharge of many guns.

Fuming, Ed grabbed a piece of carpet out of the hall and Frank quickly got out of his way as he ran out of the door and grabbed the flaming torch resting against the tinder-dry wall. Ignoring the heat licking at his hand, Ed flung it into the night. Then he began beating out the flaming wall with the piece of floor covering. Meantime, Brad Sadler was relighting the lamp. Slowly, the T Bar N men got up from their cover. Jim Daltry came in from the front room, patiently reloading his rifle. For moments the T Bar N men stood gazing at the gunsmoke-shrouded emptiness outside, blued by the shining moon. Then they turned to lean their backs against the bullet-ravaged walls and commenced to reload their guns.

It was then that Ed saw Frank running after the retreating raiders, the limp caused by his war wound seemingly forgotten. He gave out a high-pitched whistle. Ed knew that call was for Hercules, his horse. The beast was trained to respond to the whistle and he was war-hardened, used to guns. He would not be too spooked by the mayhem just gone or maybe what was to come.

It was at that moment a rider galloped out of the night from the direction of the town. Ed's first thought was that he must be with the raiders and was going after Frank and that caused his gut to clench up tight.

He drew his Colt and let loose two shots. But the range was too great to be effective. Even so he yelled, 'Behind you, boy!' But again, the distance was too great. Now, out of sheer exasperation Ed shook his fist in the air and shouted 'Damn you all to hell, whoever you are!'

Tired, drained and worried about Frank, Ed returned to the kitchen. In the lamplight he saw Carl Hollis was lying flat against the hall wall. Blood soaked the whole of his shirtfront and the floor around him. It was glistening dark in the pale yellow light of the lamp. Used to the sight of death, Ed knew Carl had breathed his last. It was then he became aware that his hands were painful. He held them up to the light and stared at them. The palms were raw, scorched, blistered. Amy came up to him. She looked drawn and tired but she said, 'Those hands need attention.'

CHAPTER ELEVEN

Fighting to contain his anger at having his remuda stolen and Carl Hollis maybe shot to death, Frank continued to run after the fleeing raiders and continued to blow his high-pitched whistle. Hercules knew those calls and, if he heard them, he would react. However, there was this other distraction behind him – the rider coming out of the night from the direction of town, seemingly intent upon latching on to his back trail.

Frank pounded across the damp grass that was silvered by the half-moon, his mind desperately seeking answers to counteract this new situation. At the moment he was running through thin brush and sparsely spaced trees but up ahead and off to his left he could see thicker brush under dark woodland. He veered toward it. The rider swerved after him.

Now sure his suspicions were correct, Frank swerved towards the large copse. Soon he was weaving through the trees and thick undergrowth, his gaze all the time searching for a point where he could hide and be unseen in order to allow him to leap out and bring the fellow down when he arrived. He would not kill him; he wanted answers, for so far the fellow had not taken a shot at him.

A place presented itself in the form of canopy-shrouded clumps of dense brush, which was amply blotched with dark, scrub-filled patches where the moon's pale light failed to reach. That would surely slow the rider down, Frank thought, and he made towards the cover.

Now crouched in the undergrowth, his Bowie clenched in his right hand and trying to suppress his harsh breathing and ignore the pain in his leg after his punishing run, Frank focused his eyes on the oncoming rider – now a dark shadow in the subdued moonlight. The fellow was peering anxiously side-to-side as his mount pushed its way through the tough scrub. However, the curious thing was: there was still no weapon in his hand.

The man was real close now, close enough for Frank to hear him quietly grumbling. Finally, there he was, adjacent to him. The smell of his perspiring horse was strong on the chill night air.

Frank leapt, his body tensed for action. Using his considerable strength he hauled the man down and pinned him to the ground. Straddling him he pressed the cold steel of his Bowie against the fellow's neck and looked into his startled eyes. 'Now, just who the hell are you, mister?' he said. 'Speak, or I'll rip you from ear to ear.'

Trying to strain away from the menacing blade the fellow said, 'Easy, suh, easy. Ah mean you no harm. Ma name is Charles Clayton Hascot and Ah badly need to talk to you.'

The name instantly brought memories cascading into Frank's mind. Hascot? Wasn't that the surname of the boy

Ed had buried alongside his pa and the boys? His stare explored the fellow's fine, aquiline features. He looked for any sign of deceit but could find none. He said, 'Go on.'

'First, is your name Edward Colerich?'

The new owner of the T Bar N shook his head. 'I'm Frank Nation, Ed Colerich is my friend.'

'Ah,' said the rider, arching blonde brows, 'then ma assumptions are not altogether incorrect.' Candid eyes met Frank's hard grey stare. 'Well, suh, Mr Colerich sent details via the mail as to the location of ma brother's burial place. He also made suggestions as to the circumstances of his death—'

'I'm aware of the details, friend,' Frank cut in. 'Get to the meat.'

Hascot looked slightly annoyed by the interruption. However, he said, 'As you wish. Briefly, the situation is this, Ah have yet to find any satisfactory answers as to who is responsible for my brother's death.' Here Hascot paused, as if wondering how best to phrase his next words. 'Generally, Ah do not believe in good fortune, suh, but who I assumed to be Mr Colerich's arrival here this noon time Ah find most providential and Ah am hoping he will provide me with further information so Ah can continue my search. Clearly Ah have made a mistake but seeing as you are riding with the group he was with maybe you can furnish me with some information.'

Frank leaned back and looked more closely at the man underneath him. He knew him now. Noontime, the fellow in the Blue Star Saloon drinking coffee alone in the gloomy far left corner during the run-in he had had with the son of a bitch still fighting that war, Kat Malling.

'John Mason Hascot, is that your brother's name?' he said.

Hope came to Hascot's direct smoke-grey stare. 'Why, yes, suh, that indeed was his full name.'

Frank nodded. 'Well, your kin is buried alongside my pa and the members of the crew that died with him.'

'Yes, Mr Colerich informed me thus,' Hascot said. 'Dreadful, suh, most dreadful and Ah wish here and now to express my condolences.'

Frank said, 'Accepted and likewise, but the man you seek is in town, though I doubt he can give you any more information.'

The Southerner sighed. 'Yes, well, Ah have now assumed as much.' He strained against Frank's iron grip and gazed up into keen blue eyes. 'Now, suh, Ah would appreciate it if you would allow me to assume a more relaxed position? This one is rather uncomfortable.'

Frank stared steadily into Hascot's calm eyes and then relieved the pressure of the knife against the fellow's jugular, got up and backed off. He slid the Bowie into the sheath tucked into his right boot top.

Standing, Hascot dusted himself down. He made no attempt to reach for the weapon pouched in the leather holster at his right side, the flap buttoned down. Instead, he raised corn-blonde brows. 'Ah think we need to talk, suh,' he said. 'Judging by the reaction of the people in the bar this noontime Ah came to the conclusion you were strangers here, and further, your accent suggested you are from the north. It was not so difficult to put two and two together. My original intention just now was to ride in on your skirmish and see if Ah could help in any way, but when I saw you chasing after those rustlers without a horse Ah came after you thinking you definitely needed help. I assumed you were Edward Colerich, but I also assumed the use of his name would open up a conversation.'

Hascot paused, narrowed eyelids now making his gaze keen and searching. 'Well, it seems Ah can be of more use to you than you can be to me, so Ah will bring you up to date with what Ah know. As Mr Colerich advised, Ah have already contacted Brock Stedman at the Lazy S for information regarding my brother. The man claims he knows nothing of ma brother or the manner of his death and knows nothing about the note found in ma brother's possession.' Hascot shook his head. 'Frankly, suh, Ah do not believe him. But he insisted he was a major in the Confederate forces and not given to lying. That claim Ah also find hard to believe. But then, during my own spell of service with the Southern army, Ah found war does throw up some strange bedfellows.'

'He ran with Quantrill,' Frank said.

'Ha!' Hascot said. His cool gaze appraised Frank's now calm look. 'Then Ah believe we are on the same side here in the search to find the killers of our relations. And Ah must confess ma suspicions are already leaning very strongly toward the Lazy S.'

'Because of his denials?' Frank said.

Hascot nodded. 'Yes. It is a strong hunch I feel.'

Frank rubbed the week-old bristles on his stubborn chin. 'Well, I go high on hunches, too,' he said, 'and I figure me and the boys should go pay Mr Stedman a visit when I get my horses back.'

Hascot rubbed his lean square chin. 'Hum, yes, the

horses and the action you were involved in at the house. It seems to me someone is getting nervy and does not want you here and for me that also points to the Lazy S.'

Frank found he was beginning to like Charles Clayton Hascot. 'Getting that feeling myself,' he said. 'Whoever took my horses just now I figure maybe took Pa's herd as well. Well, mister, I don't take kindly to folks taking my horses and shooting up my crew.' Frank paused and then added with some regret, 'Now, friend, sorry though I am to say it, I'm about to take your horse and I'll accept no argument on the matter.'

Hascot's grey gaze hardened for the first time. His hand edged toward his closed holster 'Now that's unfriendly, suh. To what end?'

'To get my horses back.'

Hascot relaxed. 'I see,' he said. 'Well, no need for such extremes, Ah will ride with you. Ma horse is strong; he can carry two. And do not forget, Ah have a keen interest in this business as well and two heads will be better than one.'

It was at that moment that there came a crashing in the bushes. Seconds later Hercules came bursting in upon them. He nickered, came forward and nuzzled into Frank's right shoulder. The horse even seemed pleased to see him.

Elated, Frank patted the gelding's neck fondly and said, 'Dammit, they sure did you a disservice when they took away your manhood, old friend, and I can only apologize for that.' After a little more petting he climbed up on to the horse's bare back and stared down at Charles Clayton Hascot.

'Are you riding along, mister?'

Hascot looked surprised, then delighted. 'An invitation Ah can't refuse, suh,' he said. He went into the bushes to where his mount was standing trembling and swung up into the saddle. 'But in this light the trailing will be difficult.'

Frank said, 'Nevertheless, we're going to do it.' He pointed into the night ahead. 'They struck off in that direction so I reckon that's where we ought to start.'

He stared up at the bright half-moon, now almost at its zenith in the star-filled sky. 'We've got the moon so maybe that'll help.'

Hascot's look was doubtful. 'Ah wish Ah had your confidence.'

'Not confidence, fellow,' Frank said, 'just blind determination. I want those sons of bitches.'

'Well, Ah most assuredly join you in that desire, suh,' said Hascot.

Not for the first time in his life Frank began to look for signs, knowing full well the search was going to be difficult. However, there was a fair-sized passel of horses in his remuda and the damp ground must be chewed up so that would help.

They both began to search diligently.

CHAPTER TWELVE

In the house in town, Amy Nation said, looking alarmed as she moved towards Ed, 'Where's Frank?'

Ed told her he suspected he had gone after Hercules.

She frowned. 'What d'you think he's going to do when he catches him?' Kind of question a woman would ask.

Ed shrugged. 'Don't know,' he said, 'but that boy'll sure think of something, he's just lost his remuda and one of his men. However, he won't put his head in a noose. He's not a fool.' Hoping he had reassured Amy, Ed now narrowed his eyelids and gazed into her calm green eyes. 'Are you all right, girl? I mean, that was sure some shindig just now.'

Amy said, 'It'll take more than that to scare me, Ed Colerich.' Now she looked at the body of Carl Hollis lying dead in a pool of blood on the floor. 'Damn those sons of bitches,' she said. 'And it seems we've lost the surprise we were hoping for.'

Ed pursed his lips. 'Beginning to doubt we ever had that surprise, girl,' he said. 'Figure Charley Hibbert sloped off to tell whoever it is we're looking for that we're here.'

Brad Sadler, pushing off the back wall he had been

leaning against while he cleaned and reloaded his Colt, said, 'Makes sense to me.'

'And me,' Amy said. 'Been thinking; maybe I can help there.'

Ed stared at her. 'You, girl?'

She said, 'I was offered a job, remember? Think it's time I took it up.'

'Now, hold on—' started Ed.

Amy raised her right hand to silence him. 'When men drink they sometimes get to talking about things they maybe shouldn't – with a little coaxing, of course.'

'And they're likely to get other feelings as well,' Ed said, 'and, for sure, Frank won't like it.'

'He isn't here,' Amy said, 'and, as I told him, I can take care of myself.'

'Yeah, maybe, but this isn't sitting well with me either, girl,' Ed said. 'Dammit, I feel I have an obligation here to take Frank's part. Why don't you stay here, help tidy up this mess?' He waved a hand at the wrecked kitchen. 'Jim Daltry's volunteered to bury Carl near the barn so he'll be around. You won't be alone. That'll leave men to do men's work.'

Ed did not get the answer he was hoping for. Amy's hand gently touch his cheek and she smiled. 'You're a dear man, Ed,' she said, 'but I'm still going. I'm T Bar N now and you'd better get used to that.'

Ed growled his mounting frustration. 'So help me,' he said, 'that boy sure took on a firebrand when he married you!'

Amy beamed him a smile. 'I'll take that as a compliment.'

'Don't,' Ed said, 'because it ain't meant to be. And, dammit, you just ain't got the clothes for vamping.'

He saw mischief now dance in Amy's eyes. 'Old-timer, you don't know women too well, do you?'

Ed said, 'No, but by God I'm learning fast and I ain't liking some of it.'

However, Amy continued to smile as she leaned over and kissed him on his craggy, grizzled cheek. Then she took the lamp off the table and turned towards the hallway. She paused at the door and looked over her shoulder. 'I'll be ten minutes, boys, OK? And, please, Ed . . . don't worry.'

'Don't worry?' exploded Ed. 'Goddamnit, girl—' Ed found he was lost for words but by using that tone of his voice he hoped he was making it very clear he was deeply concerned for her safety and that he disagreed with this whole mad scheme of hers. But she made as though she had not heard him.

He watched her leave and heard her climb the stairs to the room she and Frank had selected as theirs. Then, standing fuming in the darkness with Brad, he listened to the bumping and dragging (her trunk being pulled across the room?) that went on before silence followed. Half an hour later – that was another thing about women, Ed fumed, the incredible time it took to dress for an occasion! – she swept into the kitchen and gave them a twirl. Then, placing the oil lamp on the table, she said, 'So, what do you think, boys?'

Ed's rage, brought on by anxiety, faded. She was dressed in a sleek, figure-hugging red satin dress; cream-white shoulders were bare and smooth and alluring in the pale yellow lamplight. She also wore a layer of carefully applied make-up on her full-lipped and determined features, which further enhanced her already knockout looks. And her hair shone like burnished gold.

Ed managed to say, 'By God, girl, you've knocked me speechless.'

And Brad Sadler added, clearly equally impressed, 'Why, dammit, Ms Amy, you sure ain't the lady that rid her way down here like some wild cowboy, that's for damned sure.'

Amy looked at them coyly. 'Why, thank you, boys,' she said, 'now, will you escort me into town?'

Ed found his fears quickly returning and he shuffled restlessly in his size nine boots. Dammit, she really was serious about this. He'd thought for one hopeful moment that perhaps she had been teasing them and was dressing up to make herself feel good after the trauma of the gunfight and the death of Carl Hollis. But, he now realized, short of manhandling her and locking her in one of the rooms, he was never going to keep her here. She had decided on what she was going to do and now she was going to do it. Even so. . . .

'Girl,' he said, 'think again.'

For the first time Amy showed anger as her face reddened. She said, 'Oh! Stop it, Ed Colerich! I'm not a child, I'll handle it.'

'You keep saying that,' Ed snorted, 'but I ain't buying!'

Amy now shook her head in resignation. 'What can I do to reassure you?' Then she opened the purse she was carrying and lifted out a .41 twin-barrel derringer. 'Now, what do you say?' She looked at him questioningly.

Ed said, 'All well and good, girl, but will you use it?'

Amy replaced the gun and snapped the purse closed. Then she said, arching her fine brows, 'D'you figure I wasn't firing that Colt in earnest tonight, Ed Colerich? Goddamnit, I wounded a man and I hope I killed him!'

'No, I'm not saying that,' Ed said. 'But you're *Mrs Nation* now, Frank's *wife.* I just can't allow you to go amongst that rabble. That boy's like a son to me; I've got to look after his interests.'

Amy stared at him, clearly fuming. 'I'll remind you I'm not an *interest*, Ed Colerich, I'm a *woman*, and an independent one at that!'

'You're married now!'

'Pah!'

With that Amy turned, pulled a woollen shawl over her bare shoulders and briskly walked down the hall.

At the front door she turned and called, 'Are you boys coming?'

Brad Sadler looked unhappily at Ed before he said, 'Guess we ain't got much choice, old-timer.' Ed met his stare and growled his own frustration before ambling down the hall on bowed legs, muttering under his breath.

With the starlit night now crystal clear and further brightened by the light of the half-moon they walked down the worn, grassy slope to the Blue Star Saloon, which, unlike most other dwellings in town, was ablaze with lamplight.

About a dozen yards from the saloon doors Amy stopped in the shadowy recess of an empty shop, the door to it boarded up. 'I'll take it the rest of the way now, boys,' she said, 'but you will be close, won't you?'

For the first time Ed thought he detected a note of what might be concern in her voice and he said, 'Getting to feel you've made a mistake?'

Her green eyes flashed. 'No, dammit!' Then she squared her shoulders and said, 'Well, here goes nothing, boys.'

Exasperated Ed said, 'Nothing?' Anxiety like red-hot wire tingled throughout his whole body. 'You are crazy!'

But erect and fine moving, Amy glided away from him. After several strides across the intervening, damp ground she pushed open the right-hand door of the two upper-glazed hardwood doors of the Blue Star and walked into the warm, tobacco smoke-laden air.

She found the place was a buzz of raucous talk and boisterous laughter. Up near the small stage at the far end of the big room a piano player was tickling the ivories in fine style. A further sweep around the room with her alert gaze told her that several gambling games were in progress. A fair number of men were bellied up to the bar drinking and talking animatedly. There was also a sprinkling of strident laughter as well as jovial backslapping going on. Amy also noticed a scatter of ladies of easy virtue were spread amongst this rough-looking clientele, clearly intent upon using their God-given charms for, hopefully, generous remuneration.

All heads turned and the noise became muted when she entered. She walked boldly across the room, through the throng, head in the air and trailing the sweet heady smell of lavender behind her. She made straight to Jack O'Brian's office – she'd identified where it was earlier in the day. Without hesitation she took off her shawl, holding it in her left hand, knocked and then opened the door and posed brazenly in the doorway. 'Here I am, Mr O'Brian,' she said.

She smiled radiantly at the grey-suited, blue-cravated Irishman sitting behind his desk and apparently poring over his books. O'Brian's face lifted and lit up with surprise and then delight when he saw who it was. Beaming, he got up, came round the desk, took her right hand and kissed it. Then, still holding her hand but swinging it aside, he stood back and admired her figure-hugging, cleavage-revealing red satin dress and her creamy-white shoulders.

'Indeed you are, my dear,' Jack O'Brian said, 'and what a picture for a man to feast his eyes upon. Now, is it good news I'm about to hear?'

Amy still smiled, showing her white, even teeth. 'It is. When do I start?'

Clearly captivated O'Brian raised eyebrows and spread his hands in delight. 'What better time than now, dear lady.'

'Exactly what I had in mind,' Amy said.

But then O'Brian's face lost its happiness and became serious. He said, 'I heard you had trouble up there at the house you picked . . . shooting, your horses taken . . . a man shot dead, I do believe.' He shook his head. 'Hardly a friendly welcome to our town, I must say. And I certainly did not expect any response from you just yet because of that terrible business.'

Amy shrugged. 'Life has to go on.'

O'Brian beamed his approval. He said, 'Indeed it does, dear lady! Admirable! Such resilience! Ah! 'Tis what I admire most about America – the feistiness of its people, the go-getting attitude and the ingrained determination never to give up, choose what the obstacle.' He raised dark bushy brows. 'But first, my dear, a drink to loosen up that golden voice of yours; 'twas whiskey if I recall aright?'

Amy raised amber-red brows. 'Whiskey it is, Mr O'Brian.'

'Jack to my friends, my dear . . . Jack.'

'Jack it is.' Amy smiled some more.

O'Brian poured from a bottle into two glasses. The label suggested expensive liquor. 'Shipped in from the East,' O'Brian said when he saw her interest, 'my own small pleasure.' He passed her a glass of the amber fluid.

Amy took it and sampled the contents. She smacked her lips. 'Hits the spot all right,' she said.

'I got a taste for good liquor from those devilish English,' O'Brian said. 'I served as an officer in their Indian army for several years until . . . well, we won't go into that just now. Suffice to say there came an urgent need for me to relocate and America seemed to be the most suitable place to do that.'

'Intriguing,' Amy said.

'And hair-raising in parts, I assure you,' O'Brian said with a chuckle. 'But now, my dear, how's that voice of yours?'

'Raring to go.'

' 'Tis good to hear,' O'Brian said. 'However, first, a little theatre is required; a need to settle the audience and prepare them for the new singing sensation that is about to burst upon their miserable lives. A diva of the highest quality, and fresh from the East.'

Amy raised brows. 'Diva, fresh from the East? Mighty fine words for this wild frontier, Jack O'Brian, I've got to say. It's fortunate *I'm* well read but I have my doubts about the audience knowing what you're talking about.'

'Oh! To be sure, they'll pick the bones out of it, I've no doubt,' O'Brian said, 'as for fresh from the East? Theatre, my dear, theatre! Now, what do you intend to sing? Jim Lasker, on the piano, knows most of the popular melodies. It's just a matter of which key.'

Amy told him and, after a little thought, explained the order in which she would sing her songs.

'Admirable,' O'Brian said, 'a mixture of homely ballads, a tearjerker or two and a bawdy song to finish. By God, not only will you have them weeping into their beer, dear lady, you'll have them standing in the aisles whooping and howling like the mongrels they are.'

And O'Brian's words proved true. The medley of songs Amy selected went down well and they called for her to repeat a couple of particularly heart-rending songs. After three curtain calls she finally left the stage amid tumultuous applause. Beaming, Jack O'Brian met her in the wings and led her into the office. There he turned and, clearly ecstatic, clasped both her arms and said, 'Ha, me darlin', wonderful, wonderful! Already you're the toast of the town. But now, being the hard-headed businessman that I am, would you be returning to wow then again tomorrow night? The word must go out.'

Still feeling euphoric after her tumultuous reception Amy said, 'Why not?' Then the real reason why she was there came to her. 'But first I'd like to circulate a little, get to know some of the boys a little better.'

As if he considered he had struck even brighter gold O'Brian's eyes widened. 'Why, yes, yes,' he said. 'And, may I say, you never cease to surprise me.' Then he put a finger to his lips. 'Ach, but what is your name now? We haven't even got that far.'

'Amy.'

'Just Amy?'

'It'll do.'

'Indeed it will,' O'Brian said. 'Now, allow me to accompany you to the bar, or it will be a pawing you'll receive, I have no doubt.'

Not so, Amy found. The men were courteous to a fault, their rough, range-grown compliments flattering. The rest of the night went well and after much begging she sang two more songs to placate their need. Come midnight she was sitting alone at one of the tables nursing coffee and feeling pleasantly tired.

Despite the long ride down and the savage raid on the house and tragic death of Carl Hollis, she felt relaxed. She did have worries about Frank, of course she did; he was now her husband and dearly loved. But she also knew he was a heller with a gun; he had fought a war and had returned, so what was she worried about? He could look after himself could Frank Nation. He would come back to her again and he would find the killers of his father.

She looked around the saloon. Jack O'Brian had left her ten minutes earlier claiming he had business to attend to but that he would return within a few minutes to escort her to the house they'd picked to be their temporary home. However, what was concerning her most was the fact that Ed Colerich and Brad Sadler had been conspicuously absent. She had hoped they would have shown their faces occasionally throughout the busy night.

It was then that, what she thought to obviously be a cowpuncher, came and sat down next to her at the table. He smiled and lifted his worn, heavily dust-greyed Stetson. 'George J. Corcoran, ma'am,' he said.

Amy smiled. Was there information to be had here? She said, 'Hi, what can I do for you, George?'

Corcoran cleared his throat. 'Heard about your trouble, ma'am,' he said. 'Real bad business.'

'Who hasn't?' Amy said. Oh, dear! Was he going to talk about the weather next? But she felt she should remain amiable. So far she had gleaned little of anything that could be regarded as useful about the attack on the house, or, more importantly, who would want to do such a thing. Nevertheless, Corcoran had mentioned the fight so maybe he did have something.

Corcoran studied his scarred hands. 'I'd like you to know, ma'am, that I fought for the Union during the war and that ain't too popular a thing to have done with some folks around here right now.'

'I can imagine,' Amy said.

'But I get by,' Corcoran said. 'However, the real meat of the thing is: Mr O'Brian asked me to tell you he would be delayed, and if you can't wait it was OK for me to escort you home.'

Amy was filled with suspicion. 'Oh? Is Jack in his office?'

'I believe so, ma'am.'

'Then I think I should ask him.'

Corcoran raised dark brows. 'That's OK, ma'am. I'll go

along with you. It's right that you should check.'

It was not the answer she was expecting – not that she really knew what to expect. She looked at Corcoran. His grey eyes were innocent enough. Indeed, there did not appear to be an ounce of deceit in him. And Jack did say he was busy. Maybe it wouldn't be right to burst in on him just now, especially after he had gone to the trouble of asking Corcoran to escort her back to the house. And during the walk to the house, she could maybe pump Corcoran for any information he might have regarding the situation here in this part of the Panhandle. Words regarding events must have been passed around.

'I guess it will be OK,' she said. She picked up her large purse, felt the weight of the derringer in it and felt even more reassured. 'Shall we go?'

Again Corcoran raised his battered Stetson. 'My pleasure, ma'am,' he said. And offered her his arm.

Amy took it gracefully.

CHAPTER THIRTEEN

Ed Colerich hunched back in the shadow of the recessed shop front he was hiding in, four doors up from the Blue Star Saloon. He had sent Brad Sadler back to the house to help Jim Daltry with the burial of Carl Hollis and to tidy the place up. He'd also asked Brad to inform him as soon as Frank got back so that he could go into the Blue Star and tell Amy he had returned safe and sound. But then, he felt sure, as soon as Frank was acquainted with where Amy was and what she was doing he would do that for himself. And, no doubt, what words passed between those two hot-heads might be very interesting to hear.

Regarding keeping an eye on the welfare of the mistress of the T Bar N, he had looked in through the large glass windows of the Blue Star a couple of times during his vigil throughout the increasingly chilly night. He was not surprised to find Amy was bringing the house down, much as she had done when she sang at the hoedowns and social gatherings she attended back in Brightwater Valley before that war. But now, with a touch of irritation, Ed lifted out his pocket watch. Already, it was past midnight and in his opinion, she should have been out of the Blur Star an hour ago, maybe more. She was a married woman, for God's sake!

Grumpily, he replaced his pocket watch and glared at the Blue Star's double doors – at the yellow light streaming out through the glass panels of the door's upper sections.

Over the hours he had become increasingly bothered by this need to wait. Surely, if that wilful girl was going to learn anything at all about the situation existing here she must surely have done so by now.

Resolve settling within him, Ed finally pulled down his battered slouch hat, hitched up his gunbelt and prepared to go in there and get her out. However, he quickly drew back into the shop recess again when he saw Amy was coming out of the Blue Star's double doors. But what he had not expected to see was Amy hooked up to some Goddamned cowpoke!

He stepped out of the deep shadows and glared hard at her escort. He said in a tone that invited no argument, 'I'll take it from here, cowboy, y'hear?' But even as he said it an alarmed cry came from Amy: 'Ed, behind you!'

A bolt of anxiety shooting through him, Ed turned swiftly, clawing for his Colt. But the stunning blow he received to the head flashed bright light across his vision. Then darkness, deeper that he had ever known, grabbed him with both hands and dragged him down into its pitch-black depths.

And before Amy could react in any other way she saw another man was now coming out of the shadows. Worse, he was levelling a Navy Colt and aiming it at her escort.

Her hand flew to her mouth and she shrieked: 'No!'

But already Corcoran was stepping in front of her: to protect her? He was reaching for his side weapon but the fellow's Colt was already lined up and spitting red and yellow flame.

Corcoran let out an agonized cry and staggered back, his left hand going up to clamp against his damaged right shoulder. Blood was already seeping through his fingers as he went to ground. However, even as he fell, he was desperately trying to lift his Colt to fire at his attacker. But the fellow was already lined up on him again and fired first. Corcoran let out a groan as the bullet hit and more blood poured, clearly from a chest wound this time. Amy saw with some despair Corcoran's shot making a path through the muck of the street before slamming harmlessly into the boards of the building on the opposite side. But even with those wounds Corcoran was trying to trigger again. However, he was clearly losing bodily power and Amy watched anxiously as his weapon slowly slipped from his right hand and he settled back onto the damp soil and round horse apples. He was coughing blood and moaning.

She acted more on instinct as she reached for the clasps holding her purse shut and it was with trembling fingers she managed to open it. She attempted to pull out her derringer, but her fumbling fingers would not obey her. Meantime, she saw the other fellow was holstering his Colt and making rapid strides towards her, his hands folding into gnarled fists.

Oh! God! She attempted to depend herself by lifting her arms but his right fist was swinging upwards towards her and his left arm was contemptuously brushing aside her puny attempt at defence. The powerful punch slammed with excruciating pain against her left ear.

She cried out and staggered back but already another blow was smashing against her right eye, rapidly followed by another one that hammered against the left side of her chin. All strength was leaving her. She was vaguely aware that blood was pouring down her face and that rough hands were now grabbing her and dragging her across the wheel-rutted street. Finally oblivion overtook her.

Amy groaned as she slowly became alive to her situation. She realized that she was in a large room and that her face was severely bloated and bruised due to the beating she had taken. She was also in great pain.

Through the small window set in the adobe wall opposite her and through her least swollen left eye she saw it was coming light outside. Then she realized she was lying on a stained, battered cowhide settee and that there was the strong stench of unwashed men on the air along with the fumes of strong tobacco and whiskey. There were at least a dozen scruffy men occupying the place. Two groups of four were playing cards; one young man, she noticed, was intent on cleaning a newish-looking Henry rifle and was wearing an inane grin as he worked. And she knew him. It was the young braggart in the Blue Star Saloon who had advised Frank to get out of the district if he and his men wanted to live. She also spotted two men asleep on rickety beds placed against the far adobe wall. They were twitching restlessly and muttering in their slumber. Another fellow, she noticed, was reading a well-thumbed magazine. This one looked relaxed and confident, and appeared to be a definite cut above the rest. Most men, she noted, wore worn remnants of Confederate grey: kepis, hats, tunics, trousers and the like.

Amy tried to sit up but flopped back again, gasping as overwhelming dizziness packed with exquisite pain grabbed at the grossly puffed flesh of her face and sent blinding agony flaring across her skull.

The fellow reading the magazine looked up, laid the magazine aside, stood and came over to her. He was a burly, square-featured man with a deeply cleft chin, steel-grey eyes and a thick black moustache. What appeared to be a permanent frown creased his broad, furrowed brow. He sneered a grin as he touched the brim of his border sombrero. 'Major Brock Stedman, ma'am.'

Amy felt her stomach go ice cold. Brock Stedman? The owner of the Lazy S ranch Hibbert was supposed to have bought his beeves off and then sold on to Frank's father? He was the prime suspect in her eyes, and in Ed Colerich's, regarding the hanging of Tom Nation and the boys that rode with him.

She thought of her derringer and in her confusion fumbled around to try and find her purse. Naturally, it was not there. These men were deadly killers, not fools. Even so, despite her condition, hot anger welled up in her. She stared Stedman straight in the eye and said, 'Are you in the habit of beating up women?'

Stedman smiled but the grin expressed indifference rather than pleasure. 'Makes no difference to me, lady.'

Amy glared as best she could through her bruised eyes. 'Why am I here?'

'You are my prisoner . . . for now.'

'Why?'

'Loose ends, lady; I can't do with loose ends.'

Amy attempted to frown, but gave up as pain hammered across her skull. 'I don't understand,' she said.

'You don't need to,' Stedman said.

Now trying to ignore her pain Amy said, 'Oh! I think I do, but I reckon you are too much of a coward to tell me.'

Brock Stedman continued to smile but it was clear he did not like her questioning his courage. 'You want to know, uh?' he said. 'OK. Your husband foolishly came here to cause me trouble, is my view. And again, in my view, his father was rightly hung by me for the cattle thief he was, as were his men—'

'That is a lie,' Amy said. 'Tom Nation bought those cattle legitimately and we have the paper to prove it. You admit you killed them then?'

Stedman stared his contempt. 'A man rustles a man's cattle in this country he gets hung for his trouble, lady. Nation and his men got their just desserts. I told you, I can't do with trouble. It upsets a whole cartload of things.'

'What things?'

'Loose ends, lady, loose ends.'

Amy found her temper ratcheting up. 'Damn you, talk sense.'

Stedman glared, clearly not caring for her belligerence. 'OK, smart lady. You were brought here for one thing only and that's to entice your husband Frank Nation to come after you.'

Amy felt coldness fill the pit of her stomach. She had already half-guessed that might be the reason. What a fool she'd been not to heed Ed's words of warning. She said, 'And after that?'

Stedman smiled. 'Why, lady, after that I think it best we leave that question until the time comes, don't you?'

She looked into Stedman's brutal features through her bruised eyes. 'You intend to kill me, that it?'

Stedman's upper lip curled into a cruel sneer. 'What d'you think?' he said. 'But only after the boys have had a little fun with you; got to give them that.' Guffaws came from nearby.

'You kill me,' she said, 'and my husband will hunt down for the dog you are!'

Stedman's face returned to its mask of evil. He raised his right hand to backhand her across the mouth but somebody said, 'Easy now, Major . . . sir. Don't you think the little lady's had enough for now?'

Stedman swung round, a snarl smearing his lips as he reached for his Colt Army. But he stayed his hand as he stared into the mouth of one of Kat Malling's ivory-handled .36 Colt Navys. After he seemed to get a grip on his sudden anger, Stedman calmed and said, 'Boy, we've been together a long time but that don't mean you can continue to take these sorts of liberties. Sooner or later you're going to pay the price. You paying attention now?'

Malling held on to his lazy, inane grin. 'But Major ... sir ... you know as well as me that an officer of the Confederacy just don't behave like that toward a lady. Dammit, Major, sir, I'm only trying to preserve your intergr . . . int . . . er . . . your honour, seeing as how you want to steal a load of money and become a big important man around here . . . governor and God knows what else.'

Stedman stared long and hard before he said, 'I'm beginning to think I should have tossed you into the river all those years ago in Kansas instead of taking you on and teaching you to be the killer you are. And damn Bill Quantrill for foisting you upon me when you rode into his camp in '61 aged twelve and raggy-assed to boot. But I did, so what the hell.' He waved a dismissive hand. 'Ha! I need the john. But I warn you, boy, don't push your luck.'

He turned and walked across the hard-packed earth floor and out of the rickety door into the morning light.

Malling turned to Amy. He was still grinning. 'Now, ma'am, can I get you anything? A drink of water, maybe?'

Amy stared at this five foot four, slightly built youth with the apparently oafish grin. He certainly looked the killer Stedman said he was, though he appeared to be no more than sixteen, seventeen at the most. And most certainly she did not quite know what to make of his offer to get water. However, she also knew she would be a fool to refuse. She had a raging thirst and the metallic taste of old blood soured her mouth. 'Yes,' she said, 'thank you.'

' 'T'ain't nothing, ma'am; nothing at all.'

Then Amy, on impulse because she felt she must, said, 'You know you made a bad enemy just now?'

Malling still grinned, but Amy was now beginning to recognize there was no humour in that smile; rather, it was a mechanism to hide his deadly nature. Maybe he wanted to save her for his own ends?

Malling waved a hand. 'Oh! Don't you worry about me, ma'am, me and the major go way back. In fact he's kind of like a father to me.'

I can believe that, thought Amy.

Malling walked away to get the water.

CHAPTER FOURTEEN

The first rays of a pale sun lanced light across the range. They hit Frank Nation and Charles Clayton Hascot side on as they eased to a stop on the first substantial rise in this, until now, monotonously undulating land. Ahead was broken country: canyons, firs and black, rocky buttes.

Throughout the night both had been using instinct rather than ability, even though the two owned up to being able trackers. But from the beginning Frank had accepted their tactic was a thousand to one shot. However, from the brow of this hill, he now surveyed the broad maw of the canyon ahead; plainly the ground down there had been chewed up by the passage of many hoofs. Jackpot! Nevertheless, from this position the canyon the horses had entered looked menacingly hostile.

He turned to Hascot. 'Built for ambush, I'd say.'

The Southerner nodded his assent. 'Ah must agree. But maybe our rustling friends have now bedded down for the day after their busy night and will not be expecting visitors.'

Frank looked with new respect at Hascot. 'Certainly a possibility,' he said.

'So, perhaps we should risk the direct approach?' Hascot said.

Frank stared hard at the tall, handsome Southerner. 'You prepared to risk that?'

Hascot's pale gaze appraised him. 'Ah want the killers of my brother, suh, and if this venture will lead to that end Ah am prepared to gamble anything.'

Frank nodded his agreement. 'Then let's not delay.'

They headed into the canyon. The rising fall sun was already taking the chill out of the air, though its rays had not yet fully reached into the bottom of the canyon. They penetrated the initial thick brush they encountered by using well-trodden animal trails – cattle tracks mainly, observed Frank. As they progressed the brush became more scattered. Soon, large patches of green began to show ahead until five minutes later they came upon far reaching grassland that was sparsely populated with clumps of cottonwoods, sycamores and other greenery that was beginning to show autumn colour. Lines of trees in some places also suggested a stream.

Half a mile on, they eased up their mounts under the cover of one such copse. Now Frank observed there was a stream running through those meadows whose origins, he confidently guessed, more than likely originated from a spring. Sure enough, about a quarter of a mile ahead he saw a large lake nestling under the south wall of the canyon. Rills of water were constantly disturbing its calm, clear surface. Another thing he noticed . . . on the meadows ahead both horses and cattle grazed the land.

Also having observed the livestock Hascot pulled out a telescope from one of his saddlebags, expanded it, and put it to his right eye and began to study the animals. After a couple of minutes he lowered the glass and engaged Frank's inquiring look.

'Yours the T Bar N brand?' he said.

Frank nodded. 'It is.'

'Then you've found your horses, Nation.'

It was with more than a hint of satisfaction that Frank climbed down off Hercules' bare back while saying, 'In that case I'll take a look up ahead.'

'Before you do,' Hascot said – he paused to scan the rocky south side of the canyon – 'Ah think a man up there amongst those rocks with rifle could be useful right now.' He drew an 1863 brass-framed, scoped Henry rifle from its long leather scabbard.

Frank was suitably impressed and said, 'With that weapon, I reckon maybe you're right.'

Hascot gave him a satisfied nod and dismounted, hitched his roan to some nearby brush and then began to make his way up the side of the canyon.

Frank waited, watched his progress until, near the top, the Southerner paused, waved and then disappeared amongst the rocks. Crouching, Frank now began his scout, Colt in hand and ready.

Within a minute and hidden behind a rocky spur sticking out from the north wall of the canyon, he came upon a cabin. It was a crude, turf-built affair with a fieldstone chimney from which blue smoke was curling into the near still air.

Frank raised brows. *Well now.*

Hunched in the tall brown grass his stare probed the vicinity, but still no movement. Maybe the thieves were sleeping in the cabin as Hascot had speculated, or were eating while others were out keeping an eye on the beeves and horses?

Whatever. His excitement mounting, he licked his dry lips and with even more care he scanned the area. Then he spotted what he was looking for: one rider around two hundred yards away. He was sitting his horse in the shade of a clump of trees and was smoking a quirly. He appeared to be fully at ease, clearly not expecting trouble either from the horses and beeves, or from anything else, for that matter. Then, about half a mile down the canyon and barely discernable, Frank sighted another rider slowly making toward the lake.

Only two men watching the livestock? He found that odd and allowed his gaze to search for more, in every direction.

Still nothing.

A door scraping across hard, gritty ground distracted him. He flicked his gaze toward the sod cabin. A rough, bearded individual was coming out through the crude door and making his way towards a hole dug in the ground. There he dropped his trousers and sat on a crude seat made of stones with a plank resting across the two piles. The fellow did what he needed to do and then used a bunch of grass to clean his rear. After, he drew up his trousers, positioned his canvas suspenders over his shoulders and returned to the cabin. The door scraped to with a rattle.

The crack of a Colt from behind and the searing pain

ripping across his forearm took Frank completely by surprise. Desperately turning and rolling to his right he lifted his Colt .36 Army and armed it. The fellow sitting on the piebald mare was lining up on him again, thumbing back the hammer on his Colt. Frank fired. His shot punched a hole in the rider's chest and the fellow shouted, fell like a sack of potatoes out of the saddle and hit the ground hard. He yelped and writhed a few times before going still. The piebald mare ran off into the brush.

Tingling with shock and tension Frank stared at the cabin door, waiting for the action he felt sure must come from there. However, he heard the flat crack of a big rifle, which whacked echoes down the length of the huge canyon. Hascot? Frank stared in the direction from which the report had come. He saw the rider who, moments ago, had been heading for the lake now swaying drunkenly in the saddle and grasping his chest. Then the fellow toppled to the ground. His horse, clearly startled, trotted off towards the lake but then stopped to turn and stare at his downed rider.

Frank's gaze now searched the rocks. There high up the canyon side and waving was Hascot. Frank assessed the distance between the Southerner and the shot man must be all of three hundred yards. Even using a scoped rifle, that was impressive shooting. He looked at the waving Hascot with new eyes. He was one hell of a man to have on his side, no doubt about that.

The harsh scrape of the cabin door opening distracted him. He saw the large, bearded individual come diving out, long gun in hand. He began frantically scrambling for the clumps of brush nearby.

Frank snapped off a shot. The fellow yelped but kept moving. Another man rolled out of the door, Colt in hand, and made for the brush. Frank cracked off a couple of shots but missed. Two more men now burst out of the cabin door, ran for cover and quickly found it. Each man wore worn pieces of Confederate uniform – coats, trousers or hats.

Frank now found his heart was thumping like a trip hammer against his ribs. It was a hell of a situation to be in with Charles Clayton Hascot a quarter of a mile away and high up the canyon side amid the rocks. This could be over and done with by the time he got down here and Frank Nation could be dead.

Frank began scrambling deeper into the brush. Shots were ripping the branches to shreds around him. He aimed and fired at the Colt and rifle flashes until his own gun snapped empty. Worst, his attackers must have heard the clack of steel on steel for someone yelled, 'By God, boys, he's empty – we got him. Didn't see no other weapon.'

Frank smiled, but grimly. *That's where you're wrong, boy,* he thought. From the depths of his deep, buttoned right coat pocket he pulled out his French made nine-shot le Matt with the shotgun barrel middle around which the cylinder rotated. A formidable weapon and he knew a slight adjustment would bring that 18-gauge shotgun part into play when the cylinder was empty. However, it was with a grim face that he braced himself for the expected rush.

CHAPTER FIFTEEN

The first man to burst out of the brush had a gleeful look on his face. Frank lined up the le Matt and his lead hit the fellow square in the chest. As the blood flowed from the wound stark surprise deformed the man's face for a moment before it distorted into a rack of pain. His gun fell from his right hand and as he tottered and fell he yelled, 'Oh! God, boys, look out! He ain't done yet!'

Frank quickly changed his position and then crouched and waited, but the crackle of men breaking through brush ceased abruptly at the man's desperate scream. Frank licked his bone-dry lips. Suddenly, several shots from a repeating rifle ripped through undergrowth around him sending echoes bouncing off the distant canyon walls before fading away into the distance. Frank reacted, as only he knew how. He sent two slugs of lead whining towards the sound of the shots. He was immediately rewarded with a harsh cry of pain accompanied by a despairing howl of, 'Oh! Jesus, Nathan! Son of a bitch's got me now!'

The fellow's yell brought more lead lashing through

the brush but Frank was already snaking away on his belly to find fresh cover. God knows how he was surviving, but surviving he was and the hope he might get away with this built up in him. After all, it was down to two to one now and that could not be bad.

Settled in his new hiding place he went quiet once more. The moans of the wounded men were a nuisance but their noises were getting quieter, which suggested to Frank they were fading fast.

Ignoring the sweat rolling in thin runnels off his forehead and down his taut lean face, and ignoring the dryness in his throat, the beat of a horse's hoofs ahead came to him as a further anxiety. It could not be Hascot, he decided. He could not have reached their horses from his position on the canyon side yet. The beat of those hoofs could only mean it was the fellow who had been sitting his horse and smoking his quirly under the trees just minutes ago.

Frank peered warily through the bushes. Sure enough there he was, lashing his horse towards the eastern mouth of the canyon, *to fetch help?* Had to be. And with this clearer view he identified who the fellow was: Charlie Hibbert.

Hascot's rifle boomed, but this time Frank was disappointed to see there was no hit. But the distance must be all of four hundred yards and that would be asking a lot of any man.

Hibbert was now lost in the deep brush and Frank saw Hascot begin descending the side of the canyon, snaking his way around the huge haphazard rocks that spewed down its side to the chasm's floor.

Frank licked his lips. Where were the other two? The le

Matt was warm in his hand. He gripped it tightly and waited. The thumping of another set of hoofs galvanized him as he heard them move up into a gallop. Taking a chance he ran out of the brush and onto the open ground. The fellow was hightailing it out from behind the sod cabin, heading towards the canyon's mouth.

Frank lined up the le Matt and then lowered it. The range was too great for the short-range weapon to be effective. But the boom of Hascot's rifle told another story. The fellow yelped despairingly as he was hammered out of the saddle to sprawl into the grass. There he lay writhing on the ground, gripping his already bloody chest.

Frank stared towards the position where he had last seen Hascot. The Southerner was now on the canyon floor. He was kneeling; his right knee on the ground, his left leg bent at the knee to form an elbow rest. The rifle barrel was cradled in his left hand, stock clasped hard against his right shoulder. The gun's sight scope was still levelled on the mark he'd just hit with such devastating effect.

But Frank heard a rustle in the bushes behind him, sending his nerves tingling again – a fifth man? He dropped and rolled. There was the crash of the fellow's Colt. Dirt spat into Frank's eyes. He was firing blind now, firing at noise. Once, twice, three times. The man's Colt also barked but his shot went wide. Frantically, Frank struggled to clear his vision. When he did he saw the fellow was on the ground, still as a corpse on a mortuary slab. One of his shots – how could he be such a lucky bastard? – had hit the fellow above the nose and smashed its way through into his brain before exiting through the top of his head. Mashed up brains mingled with blood were leaking out of the gaping hole it left. The fellow's last shot must have been a reaction, Frank guessed; he probably did not even know he had fired it. The danger was over and now the shaking grabbed Frank and the sweating, which caused him to wonder how much longer his luck was going to hold out. Hascot came up, carrying his rifle in his right hand.

'You OK?' he said.

Frank climbed to his feet, dusted himself down. Already the shaking was easing off. He said, 'I've been better.'

'Your arm needs attention,' Hascot said pointing.

It was then Frank felt the pain. In the excitement he'd forgotten he'd been hit. He looked at the bullet crease on his right forearm. Already it was drying up. 'Do until we get back to Taylor's Ford,' he said. 'Right now we need to cut out the horses and get the hell out of here. That fellow running off just now could bring a whole passel of trouble down on our heads real quick is my thinking.'

Hascot said, 'Ah am in full agreement.'

'But first I need a saddle,' Frank said. 'Hercules, he don't like a man on his bare back too long, he just tolerates it for me.'

He walked around to the back of the cabin, to the corral with the rustlers' horses in it. All the mounts were marked with the Lazy S brand. Seeing the burn marks he turned to Hascot with some delight and said, 'Well, sir, guess we know who we're looking for now.'

Hascot nodded. 'Indeed we do.'

Frank then took one of the Lazy S saddles and a bridle – they were hooked over the corral rail nearby – and then walked towards where they'd left their horses. Though not tethered he found Hercules had not strayed far. Soon he had the horse saddled. He climbed up and looked at Hascot. The Southerner had stowed the Henry rifle in its long saddle scabbard. The scope must be in his saddle-bag.

Frank said, 'OK, let's get what we came for.'

The Southerner said, 'What Ah came for I believe now lies at the Lazy S.'

Frank nodded. 'I agree, but first I'd appreciate your help.'

'Given without hesitation, suh.'

They kicked flanks toward the grazing T Bar N remuda.

CHAPTER SIXTEEN

Taylor's Ford was dark and quiet as they entered it, driving the T Bar N horses in front of them. They turned the mounts towards the house Frank and the boys had selected as their headquarters when they arrived. As they approached the house Frank noticed a single lamp burned in the broken window of the kitchen.

They drove the horses into the huge barn, chucked some hay in the racks and secured the doors. Though the barn was crowded it would have to do for now. After that they walked their mounts down to the house and dismounted. Ed Colerich stepped out onto the bare back yard and met them. Frank saw the old-timer's head was bandaged.

Frank frowned. 'What happened to you, Ed?'

Ed told it all – Amy's insistence she sang at the Blue Star and her reasons for doing so, the shooting of the cowboy and then the abduction of Amy.

With the news, Frank visibly paled. Then anger came to his features and he riveted his stare onto the old-timer.

'And you let her do it?'

Ed glared back. 'Sure, like you let her come down here in the first place, remember?' He then relented and waved an arm. 'Goddamnit, boy, I did my best to dissuade her, but she's a determined lady as well you know.'

Frank fiddled with the reins on Hercules. 'Well, arguing ain't going to get her back,' he said, 'and we can only hope she's still alive.'

'Damned right,' Ed said. Apart from his first spat Frank appeared to be taking this very coolly, but Ed knew deep down the boy would be worried sick, though he would never show it.

Frank was biting his lower lip. He looked pensive. 'Never figured to be faced with a situation like this,' he said. Then he turned and indicated the tall, handsome Southerner by his side. 'By the way, Ed, this here's Charles Clayton Hascot. He's a member of the family you wrote to and brother to that young fellow you buried alongside Pa and the boys.'

Hascot stepped forward, extended his right hand. Ed took it. 'Mr Colerich, Ah have waited long to meet you,' he said. 'Ah owe you a deep debt of gratitude, suh.'

Ed waved a dismissive arm. 'You owe me nothing, mister. Least I could do.'

'Ah beg to differ,' Hascot said, 'not everyone would take the trouble, particularly since not too long ago we were enemies and still are in some places.'

Ed shrugged. 'Well, maybe you're right,' he said.

It was then Frank was surprised to see Jack O'Brian, owner of the Blue Star, step out of the kitchen. Giving him a cold stare he said, 'What the hell are you doing here, O'Brian?'

Ed laid a hand on his arm. 'Easy, Frank, because I've got some real big news for you. O'Brian here is a Chicago-based Pinkerton man.' Ed looked at Frank expectantly. 'You've heard of them. The National Detective Agency? The government used them a lot through the war, if you recall, and are still doing so, apparently. Well, the Blue Star is just a cover for O'Brian. The bald truth is, he has a warrant to hunt down and arrest Stedman for war crimes, because Washington don't believe Stedman was killed along with Quantrill in Kentucky but moved down into Texas. It was O'Brian's detective partner that was gunned down trying to prevent Amy being abducted.'

The news clearly stunned Frank. He looked at O'Brian and said, 'Is your man still alive?'

O'Brian nodded. 'Yes, but he's not well. However, 'tis the belief he will make a full recovery. That said, here's the tasty end of it. The fellow that gunned him down he recognized as being one of Stedman's outfit.'

Frank pursed his lips grimly then said, 'Well that don't surprise me.' His grey gaze now ran over O'Brian's full red features. 'You attempted to arrest Stedman yet?'

'With thirty men to back him?' O'Brian said. 'I'd be a fool to try. But I have been discreetly trying to build up a posse. However, with so many Southern sympathizers in this state it's been difficult to say the least. I've recruited only six so far. You see, to some, Stedman is a hero.'

Frank rubbed his chin. Deep anxiety was beginning to churn up in him. The raid to get the horses back, and the subsequent loss of life the Lazy S men sustained while Hascot and he were administering that lethal punishment must have stirred matters up more than somewhat in the Lazy S camp when Charley Hibbert arrived with the news. Frank had few doubts that was where Hibbert was heading when he lit out.

He set his face into even grimmer lines as his appraisal of the situation grew ever more ominous in his mind. Amy. Only God knew what was happening to her. And he most certainly could not bring himself to believe she was dead. Not only that, to hear they were dangerously outnumbered was a severe blow. He was counting on Stedman's bunch being in single figures, though Ed had warned him there could be more . . . a lot more.

He stared at the Pinkerton man and explained what had happened at the cabin in the canyon and how Hibbert had ridden hell bent out of it, at a guess, to notify Stedman what had happened.

O'Brian looked at him, his square, red face sombre. 'Well, if I know Stedman, and I think I do, he won't like that. My guess is he'll soon be coming hell-for-leather into town wanting revenge. And right now we have little to face him with in defence.'

Frank 'hummed'. His mind had not been still these last few moments. 'You know what, O'Brian?' he said. 'I'm beginning to think we're giving Stedman too much respect. How many men did you say you could raise?'

'Six, maybe seven.'

Frank 'hummed' once more and continued to hold the Pinkerton man's direct stare. 'Counting the men I have and Hascot here that'll make eleven.' His gaze became even keener. 'You know the trail to the Lazy S?'

O'Brian nodded. 'Very well.'

'You know a good place for an ambush?'

O'Brian's gaze began to brighten. To Frank, he'd seemed a man quick on the uptake. 'Why, yes.'

Frank nodded and said, 'I figure surprise could give us a big advantage, and he'll be weakened after what we did in the canyon.'

O'Brian's smile was now like a sunrise, then he rubbed his chin thoughtfully. 'He will indeed,' he said. 'And I've seen such odds defeated in the many skirmishes I have been involved in during my service with the British army.'

Frank nodded again. 'Seen a few of them work myself. How soon can you raise your men?'

O'Brian said, 'Give me an hour.'

Frank scrubbed his bristles. 'Should be enough.'

At that moment Ed Colerich coughed and Frank turned and met his grey stare. 'You got something to add, old-timer?'

'Been thinking about Amy,' Ed said. 'Dammit, boy, I feel kind of responsible, but I got an idea. I figure she might be kept at the ranch while Stedman gets on and does what you think he's going to do. Maybe, though I'm only guessing, there'll be few there at the ranch to guard her. What about if I kind of sneak up and get her out of there while they're gone?'

Frank stared at his friend and the man responsible for his and his pa's survival at the time of his birth during that terrible winter of '42.

He said, 'You willing to do that?'

'Son, I wouldn't offer if I wasn't.'

'I doubt that,' Frank said, and then nodded. 'Then it's settled.' He turned to O'Brian. 'An hour, you said?'

O'Brian said, 'Maybe less.'

CHAPTER SEVENTEEN

It was real cold, hidden there in the lower end of the rocks that formed the sides of the pass. In the chilling grey of this early Texas dawn Frank shivered involuntarily as he peered at each side of the rugged formations, trying to locate the men hidden amongst the rocks. He could see nothing; the men had chosen their positions well. No doubt most had war experience and knew the need for that. The horses were picketed out of sight out back of the west side of the pass.

The pass was about six miles out from Taylor's Ford. Frank felt satisfaction; O'Brian had picked an ideal spot for an ambush. All that was needed now was for Stedman and his men to fall into the trap. As for numbers, O'Brian had managed to recruit seven men in the short time he'd had at his disposal. And he had been generous regarding remuneration: fifty dollars a man, one hundred and fifty dollars to relatives – if they had an – should they not survive. Frank decided the Pinkerton Agency must have instructed O'Brian to use his discretion regarding payment. But with Washington footing the bill with taxpayers' money, Frank thought, exercising his cynical side, it should not be a problem.

As for Frank's bunch: there was himself, of course, then Charles Hascot, Brad Sadler and Jim Daltry, all very capable men, he knew, and deadly with a long gun, particularly Hascot judging from what he'd seen of him so far. O'Brian he was not sure about, but he carried a seven-shot Spencer .50 carbine with several spare Blakeslee tubes in a bag ready for a fast reload. The Spencer, Frank knew, was a deadly weapon in the right hands. Maybe they would pull this one off . . . .

The sun lifted higher in the sky. The air grew warmer and still no Stedman. O'Brian, who was a couple of rocks away from him whispered, 'To be sure, Nation, I expected the man sooner.'

'So did I.'

The T Bar N boss moved uneasily in his hiding place. He was beginning to suspect Stedman might have taken another route.

He peered up the pass. The small stream running through it gurgled loudly on what was otherwise almost dead silence. It was then that Frank heard the slow clop of hoofs, however, he soon realized the noise belonged to only one rider. But it was something, he thought, and he waited expectantly.

The man came into view, riding slowly and nervously and staring around him at the rocky sides of the pass. It was clear he was trying to pick out any danger that might exist there. He rode on, past the hidden ambush, apparently unable to detect anything untoward and faded out of view around the bend ahead. Two minutes later he came cantering back and disappeared around the bend he'd emerged from minutes earlier. Soon the beat of his horse's hoofs came to a stop. Hearing it, Frank tightened his grip on his rifle and licked his dry lips.

'Seems our Mr Stedman is a cautious man,' he whispered to O'Brian.

'And a dangerous one I'll have you know,' O'Brian replied in like subdued tone.

After more waiting, a group of men finally came into view and Frank did a quick count: twenty-three. At their head was a thick-set, black-moustached, surly-looking man wearing a border sombrero that shaded his square face. Frank had given the order earlier for his men to hold fire, select the target nearest them to try and avoid more than one man shooting at the same target and then await his shot to signal they should commence firing.

Blood now surged through his veins as he levelled his sights on Stedman. Cut off the head and the rest will run, so the story went, and Frank had seen such a thing happen with untested soldiers. However, his experience told him the men down there were hardened fighters; most were wearing parts of Confederate grey, which suggested they had, like him, survived more than one bloody skirmish. This would be a short, savage encounter, but Frank had little doubt his trap was well laid and that they would triumph.

Stedman's men were now well into the pass. Frank relaxed, placed the sight bead of his Henry rifle plumb on Stedman's heart. Then he squeezed into the shot but cursed as suddenly Stedman's horse shied away from something on the side of the trail that had disturbed it. Frank knew right off he had missed.

However, with the roar of his rifle the signal was given. The crash of eleven rifles now shattered the calm of the pass. Frank watched as eight of Stedman's men fell from their horses on that first volley. What followed was general mayhem: the cries of alarm, of pain; empty horses running in panic; other mounts rearing in terror as their riders desperately tried to control them while at the same time attempting to reach their weapons.

Another devastating volley rent the air and more of Stedman's men fell. Five, Frank counted this time, making thirteen now grounded. But there was still Stedman. Frank's keen gaze sought him out. There he was, heading west, out of the pass, thick dust kicking up from his mount's hoofs. Again Frank fired and missed.

Damnation!

Forgetting Stedman for now, he turned and concentrated on the rest of Stedman's men. The fire pouring down on them now was murderous and he saw two more men fall. Some were firing in return, however Frank saw his men were well covered. Clearly what was left of Stedman's men now realized things were desperate and that their leader had quit the fight. Upon that realization Rebel yells rent the air as they lashed their mounts out of the pass, riding hard after their leader.

Frustrated, Frank roared at the men emerging from the rocks around him and across the other side of the pass, 'Get to the horses, boys!'

But O'Brian was looking at him meaningfully, 'There are wounded men down there, Nation. Shouldn't we try to do something for them? I have bandages and medication here.'

His pointed to his bulging saddle-bags.

Frank turned hard eyes on to the Irishman. 'They strung up my father and his men for no reason and without mercy, O'Brian, and they shot down Charles Hascot's brother in cold blood. At that moment they made their choice. I have no sympathy. Right now, we can't waste time on them. Let them deal with it how they can for now. I promise you we will return later.'

'Ah'll second that,' said grim-faced Hascot strolling up while reloading his Henry rifle.

The Irishman hesitated, and then nodded acquiescence, though he did not appear too happy about it. 'Guess right now you have a point.'

The matter settled, Frank turned his mind to other matters. However, before going over the west rim to get the horses he made a quick head count of Stedman's men. Twelve dead as far as he could make out; five wounded. It pleased him to see only one man of the bunch of men he was leading had sustained an injury; a shot through the fleshy part of the left thigh, which, at this moment, O'Brian was now busily binding up. Even so, Frank stared at the Irishman, impatience coursing through him. 'When you're through, O'Brian.'

The Irishman returned his stare. 'You're a hard man, Frank Nation, and I suppose you're right in one way but I'll do what is needed here then follow.'

Frank set his jaw and then relaxed. 'Fair enough. We'll be heading for the Lazy S.'

'As I assumed,' O'Brian said.

Dismissing O'Brian from his mind, Frank turned to the men standing around, waiting for orders. 'OK, boys, let's go get the rest of those sons of bitches.'

Already flushed with success, the men looked keen to finish the job and followed him without comment up the pass side.

CHAPTER EIGHTEEN

An hour after dawn Ed Colerich eased back on the reins of his roan and stared down from the ridge at the rundown Lazy S ranch buildings. He'd watched who he assumed to be Stedman – squat, brutish-looking and of dangerous appearance – leave, riding at the head of a formidable bunch of men not twenty minutes earlier.

Seeing the procession Ed felt anxiety run through him. Frank would have his hands full with that bunch, no doubt about it. And now he felt half guilty about being here when the action would soon begin up the trail apiece. However, Amy's welfare and his feelings of guilt regarding her kidnap, rightly or wrongly, were still burning like a hot coal in his gut and he quickly decided he was in the right place because he fervently refused to believe she was dead, as some pessimists had been hinting she might be. And surely, even Stedman could not be so callous as to do that, he thought. But then again, *look what he did to Tom and the boys . . . .*

However, Frank had placed his faith in him and he could not let the boy down.

Ed stared again at the buildings below. As it had been since Stedman departed, the place appeared to be free of human habitation. Three horses, he noticed, were in the corral by a stream that ran around the east side of the spread. They were pulling hay from a net bag, ragged with tears. The dilapidated bunkhouse, a-piece from the ranch house, also appeared deserted. But he had this feeling in his gut people were down there, unless Amy really was dead. But that was too awful to contemplate.

Ed dismounted and ground hitched the roan. He decided the ranch house was the place to head for. He drew his Colt Army cap-and-ball and examined it. As usual it was primed for action. Now, he had to get down there. He'd waited long enough. Whatever he met he would deal with.

But the beat of hoofs held him. He stared down the trail Stedman had taken out of there not half an hour before. Within seconds, the owner of the Lazy S came pounding over the hill. Close behind him were six riders. Ed swallowed. God almighty, had Frank triumphed, or had the odds been too great and his bunch had been wiped out? Ed did not want to and would not speculate on the possibility. Right now, Amy must be his ultimate concern.

Stedman's riders drew up before the ranch house and dismounted in a cloud of dust. They appeared to be in a hurry as they all swarmed into the dwelling.

Raw anxiety now in him Ed ran down the hillside and pressed hard up against the ranch house side, near the window close to the door. He peered in through cheap glass that was thick with dust. Though dim in there he could make out, amongst the press of bodies, Amy. She was free of restraint and she was standing behind an acne-troubled, blonde-haired youth who was wearing an inane grin and, wonder of wonders, seemed to be protecting her.

Ed recognized him: the kid in the Blue Star Saloon the day they rode into Taylor's Ford; the youth who had warned Frank to get out of town. What had the little bastard got to grin about with Amy in such peril, apart from maybe he was eventually going to have his way with her?

But amazement upon amazement, the youth was saying, 'No, I'll take care of the lady, Major, sir.'

'She dies, I tell you!' Stedman roared. 'Now get out of the way, boy, we need to be on our way.'

'Can't let you do it, Major, sir,' Acne-face insisted.

To Ed's amazement the youth was still grinning and staring at the Lazy S owner, whose square face was reddening rapidly as the fury and evil seemed to build up in him.

'Damn you, Kat,' Stedman shouted, 'do it or I'll go through you! I ain't kidding around no more.'

Kat Malling still held his lazy grin. 'That'll be a little difficult for you, Major, sir, because I can beat you and you know it.'

Stedman glared. 'The hell you can! You never could! I just let you think that!'

Now Stedman was going for his Colt and Acne-face was matching him while still grinning. Two guns exploded simultaneously and Kat Malling was the one staring at his executioner in disbelief as two roses of blood began blossoming on the area of his heart.

Kat stared, more in distress than pain. 'Why, Major, sir,

you've killed me.'

'Damn you, boy,' Stedman said. He was clearly agitated and, to Ed, apparently strangely regretful, 'Ah always told you Ah could, but you never would listen.'

Malling held a hand out for a moment, as if pleading with Stedman to allow him to live then he sank to the floor and died. Ed noticed he was not smiling now but his face did hold a kind of peace.

Stedman turned to the men about him. 'Grab the woman,' he said, 'and bring her.'

Ed felt his gut writhe and his back stiffen. Amy was fighting now, but three beefy men grabbed her and dragged her towards the door. Every nerve in Ed's body was now tingling with trepidation as he drew his Colt and waited.

Stedman's men were crowding out of the ranch house and out onto the bare ground beyond.

One man stared at Stedman expectantly. 'You going to trade her, Major?'

'The hell I am,' Stedman said, 'I'm going to hang her!'

The man doing the talking stared. 'Have you gone crazy? Nation and his men are breathing down our necks.'

Stedman's Colt barked a third time and the complaining man slumped to the earth. 'You answer back to me?' Stedman roared, madness now gleaming in his eyes. 'You know the penalty for that, Goddamn you?'

Stedman put two more slugs into the already dead man and drew the other Colt from his belt then stared at the five of his men left. 'Take her over to those cottonwoods, y'hear?' he said. He pointed to the trees by the river-bank.

Ed had heard enough and stepped away from the

window. 'Not so fast, Stedman,' he called. He armed his Colt and fired once, twice.

Stedman was swinging round, a snarl on his lips. The recently drawn revolver was spitting lead but two blossoms of red were already spreading across his chest. Then it was as though his legs just gave way under him and he slumped to the dusty ground. Ed knew death when he saw it and swung his gun round and levelled the weapon at the remaining Stedman riders.

He said, 'Who's next?'

But the riders of the Lazy S had clearly had enough and were already climbing onto their horses and riding off to the west leaving Amy and Ed standing alone on the dusty ground watching them go.

It was only then that Ed felt the stab of pain in his side. He looked down. To his amazement he was leaking blood badly. Though she herself was severely beaten about the face and looking distressed, Amy ran to him and stroked his bandaged head and looked at his wound.

'Oh! Ed,' she said, 'you're hurt bad.'

'Nothing I won't survive,' Ed said. But he slowly slumped down and leaned his back against the ranch house wall and stared at the big range. 'However, I do feel a little tired.'

Five minutes later Frank and the boys dusted into the Lazy S precinct. Amy was busily trying to do what she could with Ed's wound. Frank dismounted and stepped over Stedman's body to get to her and take her in his arms. 'Thank God, you're all right,' he said and began gently stroking the blue-black bruises covering her lovely features. But Amy seemed unconcerned about her own troubles. 'I'm all right,' she said agitatedly, 'but Ed isn't. Oh, Frank! Will he live?'

Frank turned and knelt beside the old-timer. As he did Ed looked up at him. 'I got him, boy,' he said.

Frank nodded. 'You sure did, old-timer.'

O'Brian came riding in now. He dismounted, unhitched his saddlebags and came towards Frank. Then he saw Ed and said, 'This man needs attention and now.' He signalled to two of the Pinkerton employees nearby. 'You men, carry him into the house.'

Ed held up a hand. 'Hold it right there, mister,' he said, 'it's like a pigsty in there. Do what you have to do out here.'

O'Brian frowned down at the old man for a moment and then smiled and said, 'A particular man you are, Ed Colerich.'

Ed stared up at Frank. 'You going after the rest of them, boy?'

Frank looked at the thick drift of dust floating at the back of the hill behind the Lazy S bunkhouse. He shook his head and said, 'Guess we got what we came for, old-timer.'

Ed nodded and then winced as O'Brian began probing. He glared up at the Pinkerton man. 'You a doctor?'

'No, but I have tended wounds on numerous occasions. Now lie still!'

Reluctantly, Ed did as he was told.

POSTSCRIPT

They reclaimed the five hundred head that was rightfully theirs and Ed Colerich lived to see the T Bar N restored to its former glory and longer. Amy's father returned and so did her two missing brothers.

Frank and Amy finally settled who wore the pants at the T Bar N – Amy in the house; Frank the rest of it – and then went on to produce four children, a girl and three boys, thus ensuring the ranch remained in the Nation clan's hands for many years to come. Further, as Frank originally resolved, they brought Tom and the boys who died with him home to Brightwater Valley. Frank found the task he had undertaken was not an altogether pleasant one due to decomposition, but one that had to be done and would be done, by God! His father, Tom Nation, belonged on the T Bar N as did all the Nation clan. As for John Mason Hascot, Charles Hascot decided his brother should remain in the place where he died, for there was neither home nor family for him to return to back in Montgomery, Alabama.

Frank and Charles did keep in touch. And the last

Frank heard he was dealing cards in Deadwood. Rumour had it he had a reputation for being a fair gaming man but a deadly gunfighter if ever he was called.

Frank now stared up the pleasant Clearwater Valley. That damned war had ruined a lot of lives, he thought, but not all. He turned to Amy and kissed her long and hard. When he released her she leaned back and said, 'Why, Frank Nation, I do believe you care.'

Frank grinned his best smile. 'Bet on it, sweetheart,' he said.

Meantime, Ed rocked gently in his chair on the gallery and puffed contentedly on his corncob.